HORRORLAND DREAMWALK (VOL. 2)

D1287462

NOAH STEPHENS

outskirts
press

Horrorland Dreamwalk (Vol. 2)
All Rights Reserved.
Copyright © 2017 Noah Stephens
v1.0 r.1.1

Outskirts Press, Inc.
http://www.outskirtspress.com

ISBN: 978-1-4787-9048-8

Outskirts Press and the "OP" logo are trademarks belonging to Outskirts Press, Inc.

PRINTED IN THE UNITED STATES OF AMERICA

PART TWO—(continued)

INT: ONE OF Hell's circles, bright-lit by artificial light; featuring a twenty-year-old Kate Beckinsale look-alike—immediately he had carnal thoughts—who was talking and talked frequently of piercings and other body modification, whose visible flesh (desirable in complexion, texture, by association) was a sampling of such, whose body was symbolic.

Her clothing and hair, nail polish and accessories, were all bright, all the colors of the rainbow (she was as brightly colored, and perhaps as toxic, as an Amazon toad), and it served to further sexualize her, so that, subconsciously—although and perhaps partly *because* he didn't particularly like her, or didn't think much of her (as a person, on more than an animal level, although he didn't actually know and never would know her, presumably)—he wanted to fuck her really hard. He badly wanted (if he considered it, if he couldn't help considering it) to fuck her, just fuck the shit out of her, give her the best fucking of her life, ram his pulsing dick again and again all the way into her (the primitive correctness of the interlocking genitals of same-species beasts primeval as a transparent fish with the same basic facial arrangement as humans, many creatures, and capable of blue luminescence); he wanted to in a fantasy anyway. She would laugh at times, moan at times gently or gutturally, love it all the while. He would take her roughly, gently, and in between.

Auditorily he was overwhelmed, blanketed, by a teenage (or a little over teenaged) girl's piercing talk of piercings, hers and friends'; she had two belly button piercings, an absurdity of piercings, too many. Voluminous chatter. The public chatter of the electively physically modified young. Talk of girlfriends, boyfriends, alcohol overconsumption; an inane buzz

1

that filled in a manner unwanted moments of void.

Trapped at the moment in this reality, illuminated by oblong lights bright white and plastic-cased, he was experiencing restlessness, lack of repose mental and bodily.

..."Do you sometimes experience the uncontrollable urge to move your legs? You might suffer from restless leg syndrome," stated a viewcube pharmaceutical commercial. He thought of all the ailments, diseases, all the disorders of the chaotic people, the chaos of the disordered people (the uncivil of civilization). The hell of the hordes. The horror of the hobos, so many: scabbed and smelling of malt liquor (Magnum, Cobra, Colt 45), limping rot-mouthed, sometimes meth shrunken-jawed, destinationless in patchworks of rags. Considered the fact that one day would be the last day of his life, that the vulnerabilities and quirks of the human anatomy had historically been exploited, as had sexual triggers, as they were by TV (viewcube, to which brains glued).

To get out of brain, TV was best—watching shows about stupid people who seemed like a new, inferior mutation of people was better; getting lost in pap, sticking to an ass-shaped sofa cave becoming engaged in the non-problems of narcissist strangers, sentient eating yapping fucking machines, was preferable to being unconsciously lost in the mind, a slave to its negative little voice.

The viewcube declared "Dodgers win the World Series"—all were rotting, dying of decay (though tobacco, bad food, bad hearts might kill anyone first). Not an individual (in their current person-suit) was to stay. But then for some the better part of every day was a cubicle, desk, a booth,

2

a room; the blare, the vexation of humanity; filth, sickness, desolation, repetition, frustration, numbness. Many were the miserable inhabitants of the sinking stinking ship.

...He was hungover from Everclear and full-boweled working in a cubicle doing little work—and he was thinking he had restless leg syndrome, RLS, for which he did not possess the prescription-only treatment. He felt utterly undone. As monotonous moments went by he speculated that meditation was the only way through a shift here, sometimes his only effective coping mechanism.

...*He had to stop staring in the mirror.* He did not understand the dirty created world all or part of the life on which might any moment be eradicated by gamma ray, asteroid, or other reset event. The mirror showed something repulsive, an animate visual example of grotesquery. He had to stop staring in the mirror because he did not know at whom he stared. (It was a feral-looking bearded man with empty full perplexed glassy eyes. A hungover rogue, horny scoundrel, or a frightened child, lost in and outside of itself, disoriented in black reflective woods. A creature developed and under-developed, unloved and loving, unemotional and brimming with repressed emotions, needs; wanting and sad, lonely and adrift. Full of life despite cavernous eyes and early forehead lines.)

⸺⸺◉⸺⸺

Every so often he had nightmares in which a tooth or teeth broke, or a tooth/teeth were conspicuously, quickly, rotting out; in which pieces of tooth broke off with a candy bar—dreams that coincided in reality with his teeth grinding (because of fear/stress; due to sleeping pills, amphetamine, drugs prior ingested).

Many a sleeping pill made one drift closer to the oft thought and spoken of other side (which dreams were in a way a taste of), or caused one to jerk between realms, feeling again and again the slamming of the astral body back into the physical, awakening repeatedly because of being eerily, artificially put out, but feeling like some strong unknown force was responsible for the slamming sensation that had woken them, when really it was the result of waking with the dream-body out, which reflexively snapped in (the astral typically settling gently in before normal consciousness was regained).

Amphetamine could cause a manic state, mild hallucinations, might fill one with nervous energy; sometimes one's teeth clenched of their own own accord and it was not always immediately realized; one got big bug eyes with insomniac's or drunkard's purple-black half-circles beneath, and always wanted to be doing something, to be actively engaged; the mind went down illogical corridors and eventually one grew tired, tired even of their own psyche and its strange meanderings, but was unable to sleep, it would not stop running—it was a stream of images and thoughts, was always intaking and outputting much and was rendered more conscious of its dream-like river, kicked into high gear so all the more productive and craving also of physical productivity, ready for action, to do curls or read an entire book (to do curls while reading a book), if a sonata was on the radio attempting to guess each next note of it; would many, many hours later, strung out, stoned but still switched on, be trying to make sense of or read into a children's cartoon (all of which always seemed intentionally quite bizarre, the whole of which seemed to grow more bizarre with years), seeing outline apparitions and perhaps becoming conscious that the organism had been speaking nonsense aloud, alone, to itself, that the stream had become insanity or typically was insane (a word that could not be accurately applied) but was making a kind of sense, any elaboration on which would have been more nonsense, as the sleep-deprived, drugged up bone-hung meat-sack paced while quasi-thinking, quasi-dreaming, a relatively big-brained organic machine that bode behind walls.

———— «◍» ————

One day Henry took a Paxil, a Paxil that had recently expired, and walking in sporadic rain he felt he sensed the individual raindrops, knew in advance the trajectory, precisely, of passing vehicles. He was seeking and unable to find the community clinic he'd passed many times that provided sliding-scale services to local unfortunates, the maladjusted, chemically impaired, the addicts, freaks of nature. He decided finally in desperation to attempt to see a psychiatrist in a building that housed the offices of two; waited long minutes alone in the antiseptic-feeling waiting room, vaguely hearing a female patient talking to one behind a wooden door; at one point to his astonishment the pattern of the multicolored rug he looked down at absently with his head low, between his hands, began to swirl and would not stop, but he knew it was only his perception. The psychiatrist came out, gray-mustachioed and -bearded, seeming kindly, who had been in a session with the woman. "What happened?" he asked amazed-looking of a Henry who must have been visibly insane or deeply distressed. Manic laughter was the reply, interspersed with mockingly repeating the question, as he went out the door and down the steps, the shrink watching him. (He did not think why he had come, nor did it occur to him he might have spoken to the alienist.) He headed, in a sort of nervous fever, toward the university library to obtain the clinic's address from the internet, but as he approached it from the courtyard he became again conspicuously crazy or more crazy; he had begun to freak out because of the number and proximity of human beings through whom he had to pass, who were in no way altering their pace or course to accommodate him (as if he were a ghost). He briefly felt engulfed by docile but discourteous similarly aged and attired members of his species and was dodging them, terrified-eyed, perspiring profusely. They all seemed of the same mold, were somehow all too brightly-clothed, natural and ordinary yet more inhuman than human, seemed like movie extras or incredible holograms of dull beings. He was momentarily, at the worst time, in the midst of people walking in all directions in groups and singly who (as usual) he couldn't bring himself to make eye contact with and who seemed generally unaware of him; and hurrying to pass in front of a pack of female collegians so as to not to be stepped on the girl at the head of the group said with a growly undertone "What the fuck?" quite clearly and probably stopped to watch him moving, sweaty, panicky, through the horde. But he, of course, did not turn to look at her, had hardly seen her as he rushed by almost making contact with her.

<hr />

To be of the living dead might mean one liked skeletons sexually, or rote actions, routine days; prisonesque environs—physically, of the mind. Girls young with black-makeuped light-less eyes bringing tractor-beam death-life to alabaster visages of slight cheekbones. Slim-legged visibly in tight tapered jeans, with black pupils within brown irises that pierced from the center of circles of black eyeshadow.

<hr />

Night, fragments...nocturnal people with stink worse than one's own, bigger bags full of can money for drugs, booze, food. Hopping over floating past soiled worn faces, skin; grizzled people hauling weighty loads with ashy ghost appendages—displaced people leading lives of hopeless routine.

It was routine, habit, their will to keep at the old survival game (no fun), each day much like the last: pacing, contemplating, sizing up; holding for alms paper cups in subways, their tunnels, various crannies of the tireless mean city among its unsympathetic yuppies, unaccompanied and in clusters, some on route to whine or returning from complaining to fraudulent friends about everything (and nothing) but the puzzle they cannot mention it lurks within too deep inside—just clothes and chemically conquered hair cutting the low sky and stomping on the spirit of anything fundamentally human out of a sense of their superior humanity, caring superficially about their nothing somethings. Fucking animalistically and then touching up their makeup, hair still coitus-frizzled but gotten to before work on Broad Street. Subtly it came out—little hints of repugnance from the other side..."slit your throats," the bum said as they passed, perfumed pretty packages. The observer nodded secret agreement before, bitter, scurrying back to underground, asking a cigarette on the way from pot sellers in the park, it just now no longer quite dark. (Beauty, a smile, coming on with the light.)

———•((•))•———

A journey through the dark...lusting after the daughters of aging men (failures, procreators, hard workers).

Sitting at the card table in the mechanic's garage he (Henry) sat thinking about the daughter of a short over-the-hill man—both of whom sat at the table and were small-talking with him (the man in Thai, the girl in English), the father drinking with him—thinking about her red-lipsticked lips, youthful handfuls of breast, braces, long lashes, budding beauty, alluring feminine smile, thin virginal legs that led to earthly paradise; imagining the heavenliness of performing cunnilingus on her, of juice the sweetest.

Imagining being inside her tight pussy, her moaning beneath him. Pseudo-seeing her mouth open eager to receive semen on her pierced tongue.

Into the dark recesses of mind... She was playing with the metal bar in her mouth, and when she saw him looking smiled what seemed a flirtatious, even knowing smile. And he thought of her taking his engorged cock gratefully into her small warm mouth, fantasized about her perfect vermilion-painted lips being around his hot erection, that he felt the metal along the shaft as she looked up with eyes approval-seeking and equally lustful; imagined his dick going through soft lower lips and entering her fully, the fit glovelike and right. He thought of young women shuttering on his cock, vaginas clamped tightly at its base, nipples hard and sensitive on bouncing b-cups—of one doe-eyed and intelligent with a sweet disposition in complete physical ecstasy that he was causing her...in the below-the-surface world of animality, carnality.

———— «◉» ————

Henry in a room somewhere in China was thinking: *I'm just an invisible, ineffectual little drunk. A failure, miserable. I want to be killed, be run over by a car and die. I have no one. I'm alone—staring at a bare hotel bed in an empty room, uninhabited even by me. Unloved. A low self-esteem drunken psycho. Worthless and purposeless, another good-for-nothing blob. Bones, blood, meat and water. My life has escaped me, in its place is a trudging on; I must have missed the point. I'm Mister Cellophane. "Should have been my name, Mister Cellophane." A ball of repression. Impotent. Incapable. Unwanted. Unknown. Undeserving, and every day less desiring, less believing, less feeling, emptier, everything emptier. No one pays attention, no one wants to know; no one should blame them. I drink cheap beer, smoke cheap cigarettes, and watch TV. I have become no one.*

<hr>

The nature of the hole (of Hell, Earth—hot blue planet hidden (its inhabitants unaware of outside creatures more than the other way around) in an incomprehensibly vast vacuum, void: the enigma of space, speckled throughout with entities at monumental distances) was dampness, grayness and grime; and somewhere in the drain, deeper than the cruel similar-looking creatures who might have been androids, drones, was *he*, immortal *I*, a confused entity confined to a pit made worse by its disoriented animality. An abyss abstract and theoretically bottomless, an awful infinite cistern.

The hole was not a place, except that in this case it was Earth-set; it was a deleterious state of mind, more accurately spirit; it destroyed one in darkness surely and often indiscernibly, even enjoyably; it was a fall down a wide well, a plunge always downward that felt like no motion, maybe like sleep (because of the loss of time and bearings), possibly the only eventual end to which was, so to speak the only bottom being, the expiry of the wretch (the passing on of a energetic entity that could not be destroyed).

10

With some people, practically nothing could make them momentarily happy; anymore there was just about nothing they liked. They lived emotionally flat sorts of existences (nonexistences of a kind), conscious of the monotony but their routine hardly bothering them anymore, no longer mentally exerting themselves any more than they had to to stay alive; and they were usually friendless, little relating to or seldom thinking of most people, which was doubtless a significant reason for their chronic aloneness. One such man for example, in his twenties in the initial decade of the twenty-first century, besides regarding his life as a day-to-day dullness (excitement-less, eternal-feeling), found most people boring, masters of mimicry, preferred solitude and solitary pursuits, perhaps was an anchorite born. Nonphysically necrotized, his life was a blur of empty twenty-four-hour blocks, its soundtrack the din of his workplace, traffic, TV most of all.

The alcohol was gone nearly and a eulogy had been composed. It went: So long liver, so long life, if only there was more stuff of sickness (to make sicker the sick sick-world-born, to hasten the end); the lucidity, lessening of inhibitions and inner burn it causes are much liked.

———————•◦(◦)◦•———————

A problem arose when one no longer saw the point in their own continuance, when they continued with no desire, without any wonder, neither grateful nor glad, but only out of habit, because of their animal nature (because they yet remained alive, the organism wary of its extermination)—insomuch as it was problematic to be extent in a conspicuous void.

———————•◦(◦)◦•———————

Among adults some spent most of their free time, their superfluous money, in bars—locked in a cycle, talking mostly to those they'd see there; when disinhibited enough trying to pick people up and occasionally succeeding, even if it typically wasn't worthwhile, and if a relationship developed it never lasted, would be looked back on as a waste of time (generally), a waste of time like all the hours spent in bars, hoping, waiting for something, maybe a new form of death or one long unexperienced.

Some spent their entire adult lives locked behind bars of steel; and it seemed a bit barbaric and unusual, a failure of an idea rehabilitatively speaking—besides which it was preferable for prisoners to be unaware of their lack of freedom, all the while being productive, not of course for themselves so much as for masters. (Had rehabilitation ever been the goal? Or just to box away out of sight the misbehaving animals, animals who would perhaps gain a gang and accumulate tattoos in their place of relegation, who would maybe commit their first homicide and/or become homicide victims, might feel for themselves the simultaneous shock and entry of a foreign object into the body's delicate internal machines (pumps, filters, constructors). Creatures who would find a clique, learn the internal barter system, all the culture and procedure; take common routes to institutionalization, throughout their incarceration being observed and tended by creatures of the same type who sometimes were as violent but lived some of the time outside the barbed wire (where, often, they had families that maybe gave them a sense of fulfillment, wives who maybe fucked them).)

Grotesquery could be: a substantial part of the species, having lost its sanity, frame of reference, shuffling collectively toward the word's embodiment—an outlandish, unpleasantly distorted humanity, puppetmasters responsible for their abnormality, enslavement, puppeteers who were not easily recognized or satisfied, who were not even contented by subjects fully conscious of their serfdom and nonetheless thankful for their being permitted and supported in a pitiful existence.

Evidence of an advanced decadence, humanity rotting from within, was readily apparent in Babylon the new, where all the advantages of great wealth were longed for by the plebs, which eagerly kept apprised about the rich, famous and stupid they revered; where refuse (living, inanimate) and decaying matter were everywhere to be found and forms of decline were everywhere exuded.

While those unaware of their deadness felt better, day-to-day life was an extended sort of death for the special dead, the spiritually dead or exhausted who walked or drove the streets of the land that fetishized celebrity (a phenomenon which was a result of fetishism), technology, and instant-as-possible gratification; also murder, sexual assault, and violence in general.

News was always the same. People robbing, raping, shedding the blood of intimates, acquaintances, strangers; people young, middleaged, old dying in myriad manners. Some of the young the deceitful bully's peons, military in the Middle East—where sometimes, sometimes often, the bodies of people of all ages, civilians, were unexpectedly exploded in all directions (choke of black smoke; rain of gore, fat, shit from intestines deflated snakes, tattered clothing, bits of possessions, products). Where, sometimes, blown up without any forewarning were people in markets, in front of mosques, on sidewalks, in crowded buses, at packed celebrations, people black-clad at funerals (and as the smoke ascends black shreds raining with blood, brain, flesh down over corpses and the living (ordinary, moments-ago-intact), wandering disoriented, hands to bloody shirts and screaming from the ground, stumps pulsing with a pain never known and cauterized or still gushing).

On TV celebrities broke up, got together, broke into activism. People parodied themselves on reality shows that there were hundreds of. Commercials (aired four times an hour) were just as loathsome and unreal, as were loud, expensive, intellectually numbing movies, their imagery more than ever more engineered than genuine.

New and faster devices, gadgets, were developed, put on the market. New fast food chains were incorporated; new restaurants were opened, mattress stores, appliance stores, rent-to-own, electronics, furniture, auto parts, department stores. There, everywhere, were failed businesses, resultant empty buildings left to crumble, rat-inhabited structures abandoned homeless people were sleeping at noon hungover in the shadows of; they were situated in large gray lots in the cracks of which were oft-trampled weeds striving sunward and being killed by the sun and far-traveling mission- and scent-driven ants, ants that lived below the fractured concrete. There was an abundance of the displaced and desperate; were permanently tan, dirty mephitic bearded fortysomething shopping bag-toting Promethean men with lifeless eyes, scabbed weather-beaten cheeks and lips, who slept near coypu in tall grass riverside.

There was...a big asshole drunk in a baby blue ball cap about fifty with eyes baby-blue too and a blotchy red face and rough skin; a man who had worked construction most of his adult life and was currently a homeless burnout with gray stubble and a protective, huskier son he frequented bars with. Sitting near a tavern they were about to go into they presently passed back and forth a thirty-two-ounce Gatorade bottle filled with vodka and watermelon pulp, the seeds that slipped past them going undigested through their insides. They occupied a public bench of wood and green iron and the dad, already visibly intoxicated, gave a good cold stare to pretty passing young women, stared with obviousness that seemed exaggerated at their passing tight-clothed asses, sometimes loudly remarking on the objects of his lasciviousness in a way indicative of his sickness, his many sicknesses, all being the same.

————◄(◕)►————

The man who chose the road less traveled his fingernails were all chewed up, some of the cuticles bloody; he ate the white strips of nail sometimes that he bit into small pieces after ripping them off with his dulling, eroding, yellowing, imperceptibly cracking, browning, eventually even blackening, becoming painful, unusable, falling out, away, cavity-ridden teeth (and he wondered whether he irregularly experienced a certain internal pain because of this unconscious consumption of fingernails; whether he would later, if he could not or did not remember to put a stop to his habit, have hospital trouble, die of a belly full of fingernail bits, decades' worth trapped within, die like someone with pica). His hands yielded a bounty of insight, from palm lines to scars, each a story (but who cared about the stories—anymore rarely did he)—but did they yield insight into his pathological nail-biting? Was it a symptom of the stress of the organism, this particularly creatural creature in the nonbiological mechanism; just

16

a behavior carried over from childhood? In important ways was this individual, example, not mechanical enough for the mechanics of its circumstances, not enough to play success-fully—to sufficiently adapt or appear adapted? Was it best it was incarcerated, splayed, dug around in? Deprived of mo-bility and turned to feces-flinger, became fodder for police state police shows of the reality genre (being apprehended time and again, as a camera rolled, while shirtless, bloody and drunk)?

———(())———

One man, an alcoholic, had for a decade lived check to check, never being able to save (by going sober)—in order to get the fuck away, pay debts, buy a pair of jeans (because all those he owned had holes in the seat of them and else-where). Ate a lot of bad food like ramen, viewcube dinners, bland sandwiches of preservative-packed grade-d meat con-glomeration on corn-syrupy white bread; always bought the cheapest available bottle of wine, which made for a better night than one without; lone and lonely drank the bottle sur-rounded by blank walls, secondhand furniture, and an invis-ible cloud, miasmic, of chaotic thoughts; was underemployed and found odious the minimum-wage paradigm-enforcing propaganda-reading job he spent four to six days a week at. Felt devoid of hope, aspiration—unfree, that he lacked op-tions. (Felt that he was living in a recklessly capitalist to-talitarian society, the Illuminati (like a bunch of wizards of Oz behind a curtain) the supreme puppeteers of people the world wide; a society in which misfiled or erroneously filled out paperwork or an insufficiently protected electronic identity might mean one was fucked; a dog-eat-dog society that was correspondingly anti-intellectual; a society of the people always coming last; of wage slavery, in which the new slave was an economic slave much better provided for, more comfortable, complacent than those of old; an evident class society in which it was impossible, at least implausible, to ever get out of the financial hole if one ever got in it; a society most members of which were under the veil.)

———)((●))(———

Nightmare time—starring the people intangible. A dream, true, within which one had many dreams of different sorts (some dreams inside other dreams), that was only a nightmare depending on mood, which depended on happenings and one's responses, which could be a lovely dream, all of it always a dream, an organism's life on a habitable planet. A dream, abstract and tragicomic.

———)((●))(———

He knew, had known, a general hatred of people (an emotional response unfortunate); the feeling of nothing, truly (outside of physiology, time and place), in common and few things commonality desired in with the bulk of the masses (of the masses nearest him, that he was trapped among); the feeling of being crushed and ignored by them, misunderstood and disliked, ostracized, deemed lowly—and he become disassociated enough from most that they became large annoying or mean-spirited flies that he avoided, that were largely predictable; as many had he came to find time alone more rewarding, stopped wanting to be liked, be homogeneous in appearance and behavior, stopped wanting to achieve in the eyes of others or ever again be in a committed relationship. He would, if he wanted, surround himself with books, trash, or strange graffiti.

———◦((◦))◦———

He'd come to think of sex too much perhaps, maybe become sexually obsessed, in part because of his lack of coitus during most of his sixteenth through nineteenth years and during spans of later adulthood, in part because of periods of promiscuity (but probably not due to his feared inability to love or, in his perception, love's being always thwarted, even if always self-thwarted (self-thwarting being what many people's entire lives were histories of, probably some of their prior lives), or deep down not believing in love); due to probably more than anything else pornography, consumption developed to addiction; because of its sort of grossness (deadness—like something natural rendered unnatural; like a coyote dead with its long pink tongue hanging out, its guts wide open, pink in red, strangely, finally, contorted under sudden headlights). He'd come to experience ever-going emotional and sexual longing; terrible fixations, ideation. Came to feel there was nothing to care about, but the end (when what there was was everything); no reason to live other than being hardwired to, in the habit of doing so (it'd always been hard anyway); to outlive more fools, to be a fly in the ointment, or to improve if ever so slightly genetic selection.

⸻ ((●)) ⸻

Horror was...pinned up, pasted on—stench of dung, rooms with peeling walls, don't-want-to-breathe unknown chambers. Under disparate layers of wallpaper disturbing poems in chicken scratch or carved; oblong packed closets never noticed for their secret history (which told stories seemingly intentionally) but that by flashlight one night finally were— their walls papered with decades-old newspaper articles, Bing Crosby's son suiciding by shotgun, a Winchester ad adhered with yellowed paste. (And there were rustles then as if of time itself; one shook with the dark inner, smelled mothballs and decaying clothes—some in decomposing zip-up plastic sheaths, in drycleaner's bags new fifteen years earlier.) Biker chicks with eighties hairdos wearing studded leather jackets over red, white and blue leotards fellating German shepherds in Lamborghinis; a fourteen-year-old raping a seventy-five-year-old at knifepoint in her home, on her living room floor. While on the TV (in, except for sun diffused by orange ceiling-to-floor curtains, an unlit den at midday) cartoon characters made of taffy were line-dancing and singing against a static pastel background (of oddly, simplistically shaped trees and hills) a fifty-six-year-old man fondling his grandniece—eleven and with Down's syndrome—whom he is babysitting. Westerners on the countrywide battlefield of a war that wasn't protecting their other-hemisphere homeland's so-called freedom—a war that made the heimat more hated—getting shot, beheaded on the web, drooling or gushing blood after death. Ten thousand Iraqis dying like animals too.

In the desert, which never took prisoners; everyone essentially was the same, as demonstrated in death. Interchangeable and black-red bleeding, all comprised a dysfunctional family expanding to the brink of collapse, a family of which some members felt it was best to be an outcast.

There were cases when (for example) their world could be collapsed to a pinpoint, along with the entirety of matter. A blade of grass could never fully be understood. Birth and death and sleep were infinitely complex even at the hour of humankind's highest development, scientifically, in millennia, as were bacteria, and filaria, nematodes.

Did nematodes kill and torment one another as did the self-regarded most advanced animals on Earth or did they only seek the hostship of other organisms, sometimes large as well as oblivious, fluid-filled corpses-to-be?

———————⊂«◉»⊃———————

The monster passed out soused in the bathtub at his friend's house (Henry, holding a nearly empty beer can) was discovered as a dime-sized spider crawled down his forehead and into and out of his open mouth. And soon his eyes, dead, came alive again, still deathly, the gray-blue of an overcast impenetrable sky...

I am a seriously fucked person, Henry, semi-drunken, solitary, somewhere different, was thinking. *Especially when drunk, which—as with everyone—makes me a different person, a different version of myself. And when I am drunk—a task these days, I'm not near yet and don't like to be drunk—I will sometimes play the buffoon, like the tragic actor on the stage of the world. I can have problems with self-censorship. I am not dinner party material. I am not uncontrolled, but I might be, and without even internal forewarning, but am an animal. I have antisocietal thoughts of a non-ohthatsnormal sort. I am broken and rebroken, a sad organic repercussion of millennia, cells regenerating every seven years...and maybe I'll be dead in seven years. I am plain-clothed, unassuming—but who am I anyway? The what is the same thing as everyone else; ambulatory and amazing-brained evolution. And raccoon-eyed, and assuming guises necessary but lurking, me the monster in the tub, wet and heavy and slumbering from drink, found mouth ajar, and just then a spider crawls across my forehead and in and out of the oral oval of the self-stupefied. The self-pretending, self-uncomprehending. The whiskey-soused destructor. Joker, smoker, toker at midnight; a nice guy, though it might be a lie, or just not the case in a given instant; hard-used, hard-living, and, in America, hard-pressed. My prognostication: in middle age this weighty spirit probably will let go the heaviness; not infrequently I don't know if it's worth the wait. I need religion or a woman—not primarily for sex—and can find neither. Come to think of it a little purely carnal coitus would probably lift my spirits. 'Cause I'm down, down low; I guess that's the road, but I wonder as seconds tick how far it'll stretch. 'Cause I'm vomit-man, lowered-standards-guy. Ephemeral, evanescent Mister Cellophane. Coulda been my name—ephemeral, evanescent Mister Cellophane. e.e. cellophane.*

———— ((◉)) ————

All seemed so placid in their comfortable domestic pairings—as they strutted about, from store to store, down lanes aimless. Untouchables unmemorable, perfectly socialized; superior yuppies, their clothes, accessories, demeanor proclaiming middle class.

He saw, was contained (but could not interact) in, a zoo full of less-than-intelligent animals, certain of which sometimes saw something realer than the illusions, the monotony, shallow ritualism, that passed as their lives (lives of propagation, accumulation, emptiness, deterioration); saw someone with a wooly beard, a stench, a battered face mumbling to themselves; who, garbed in contrasting soiled secondhand clothes or little more than rags, passed sluggishly by, brushing one of their shoulders; who clearly wasn't of them—a person, considered now a nonperson, that had been excreted by the herd after being thwarted by the system and anymore was a part of neither; who was just excrement, the disposable and the disposed; bacterial poo under society's shoe. Precariously surviving shit ignored and resented, unknown, categorized automatically like everything (all could be reacted to but nothing understood). Pregnant with farts, alcoholic and cirrhotic; with a cholesterol level that was high and eyes that were bloodshot; unloved, unfuckable and wretched. A person who had become a thing; one that most were averse to, felt themselves different from, maybe feared. Who was like any of a number of living wretches defecated by God and stinking of waste and malt liquor; that were malnourished, whiskered, open-sored and spider-bitten; that had track-marked arms or the shrunken jaws characteristic of longtime meth users, and who were perhaps still using, six straight years after their first hit. Living feasts, sun-browned, for cruelty and sorrow. People that could have been anything and had become lowest caste; who lived in shit, smelled of shit, were shit; who had reached the point where all they wanted was some drugs, all the time.

On desert isles spiders and land crabs scurried to the sand from the vaginae of obese corpses of the recently dead. The malodorous bodies, halfway there already, would come to resemble deteriorating human-shaped transparent trash bags filled with stinking brown-purple putrescence like mashed prunes and swarming with writhing sun-baking maggots, at the upper end of which were yellow-white teeth the gums and lips eroded from them, bulging lifeless eyeballs of yellow ooze, and a matted mane, shoulder-length—brown or blonde, black or orange.

They were the decomposing shells of dumpy women (many of whom produced fat fuck-up additional humans) who, in life, when their bodies were kinetic and soul-harboring, before the end of their time of change, of learning (or

24

lack thereof), their short sorrowful spans, had produced an depressing internal monologue that transcribed would have filled a library; done plenty of eating, secreting, gossiping, judging; fucked fat men, complained, and on viewcube—called colloquially the idiot box for more than one reason—watched programs about better-off, societally sexy strangers complaining and fucking other societally sexy strangers; kept abreast of celebrity romances, new mainstream American movie and TV stars, the lately lionized; and hardly ever pondered their existences, their lengthy spans of somnambulism in the material realm.

⸺ ◖◍◗ ⸺

He saw dead babies in heaps in dumpsters among an assortment of empty product packaging, of things purchased that were now worthless; bloody tampons; used condoms; sundry garbage, miscellaneous debris of the human disease—all of it scurried through by otherworldly hot-tempered mutant rats with long slick segmented tails, oily feelers, long sharp yellow fangs in demoniac tapering gray faces lit by red ruthless eyes. The miniature cadavers—of which the never-opened eyes were tight-shut—lay atop, were sprinkled with other inanimate refuse, contortionist fetuses in permanently suspended animation, in various stages of decay; were the colors of bruised fruit, traumatized flesh; were the bodies of people who, while never having really lived, had experienced a few minutes of misery, and whose faces in some cases (frozen at the moment of death) were records of that misery.

25

Across the street there was an almost soundless explosion of blue luminance, followed by an electrocuted man— a man who had been working on a transformer—dropping from the bucket at the top of the crane he'd been situated in and hitting the ground with a thud. His body, rendered immediately lifeless by the fatal jolt, had been partially deep-burned in the long moment's burst of alien blinding light; and his surprising, horrifying demise had been an event somehow more lifelike than the life sleepers wake to, though it may have been a dream (the observer, a child in a dark living room, could not with certainty remember).

He saw people with ingrown toenails, chewed down painful fingernails (so rendered in an altered state of aimlessness and nervous energy by someone self-anesthetized and subconsciously self-hurting); itchy sexually-transmitted rashes in areas awkward that never went away. Saw a homeless man about fifty shadowed by beaten ball cap with nothing in the world but his physical presence in it who watched people in their lit living rooms from the sidewalk—silent, motionless; thinking unknown thoughts, perchance thoughts of longing, envy or hate, as he followed the actions of strangers whose lives were so familiar yet distinct from his.

Fantasies might become madness, badness. An important gulf could close between dreams potentially injurious and "reality" (and as it closed one was too close to the smeared mascara, to the placeless painted-over walls), desire and disgust, imagination (with all its chaos), burst through like frenzied mercury. The mind could be a boundless demon, unpredictable, uncontrollable, sick-making, maleficent.

It was an amusement park of sights and thrills, where illusion had to do for actuality. A kaleidoscope reality of, when faces seen, visages mostly mean or impassive, among them old Orlan's—hair white-touched; mug, particularly the forehead, visibly lined, an expression of cynicism etched on it—and mindtrapped and waylost Henry's (Henry the other version or earlier incarnation of the elder man).

It was...a darkened room, the blinds down, on a pleasant March Sunday afternoon. Cheap cigarette papers, high-in-mercury tuna sandwiches were on the table; classical came from the radio, tuned to FM; a man was reading late nineteenth century literature featuring an antihero as alienated and young as the sad, dark-eyed soul marking time (to little purpose) in this unadorned room in imposed and self-imposed solitude, privation (if companionship, love could be said to be necessities of life). He, pallid and unshorn, was undergoing entropy in a void now-bright now-dark, was homegrown and shunned, a unique failure. Such a figure ailed, fighting to restore confidence and drive after so many defeats.

⸻ ((◉)) ⸻

It was like being in a wasteland—so much because it was one. Half-dead (mostly spiritually) in one of innumerable corporate slaveholds were the new slaves, drones whose lives outside of work were as dull and dispiriting as their jobs—the modern-day serfs, barely sustaining (perhaps by and large less happy than those of old); coming home to marijuana or if not with wine, to generic peanut butter on store-brand unhealthful white bread. Getting by well enough perhaps for the living room staple to receive seventy-plus channels airing advertising and programming partly entertaining, partly confusing, partly repulsing, and partly intentional lunacy—all of it a mirror pointed at a cracked society. A society of which some members, dehumanized daily, resided in the large cracks stubbornly, perilously surviving (out of habit, strength of will)—doing so only for the hope of better days; with access to health care only at the cost of great debt. Doing so without meaningful relationships (maybe without sexual intercourse), without attachments or enriching avocations;

doing so drearily in desolation amplified by invisible waves and disembodied, metallic voices, by the speech and images of strangers as characters coming from a bright electronic box.

--- ((•)) ---

For the happy herd animals—he had contempt. Had disdain for the better part of those people, the majority, who were so easily able to comfortably function in surroundings familiar to them—in the society of which they were so representative, in complacent pairings—while certain others seemed predestined to become, slowly, sullen onlookers: adjusted for the worse little-loved adults who didn't understand how to or were no longer fit to belong; who were apart inalterably, were regarded at a glance or upon acquaintanceship as strange (in some way, maybe an unidentifiable way) and thus became more so: more abnormal, ill-spirited, contemptuous; sicker with the sickness that was already being reflected back.

Outcasts were being daily forged, shuffling along in the cold with runny noses or stuffed sinuses, with sore throats or fevers; bitterly looking on overdressed in shabby clothes on bright summer days. Observing the comparative bourgeoisie—those they had been rendered different from, rent from; those who were upset by the spitefulness they perceived in the eyes of the near-nonentities when they passed them sitting on the sidewalk—with coldness equal to or greater than that of the hearts of those they detachedly studied.

There would be showers and many sequential similar days; a blur of time dispiriting. Grayness and clouds, high 'round fifty-two. Madness stirred aloud in his veins that were like tangled yelping vines. He sat on a patio in a lawn chair staring at the droopy greenery of the plant he faced or, in a different year, stood there looking up at an early-afternoon sky.

He thought of poisoned waters, fish floating dead in sebaceous seas, soil nevermore cultivatable, mushroom clouds and pestilential fog. Of dry rivers, widespread sustenance and water scarcity, toxic air and food; of civil unrest in every state and steep rises in developmental and mental disorders. Of rising oceans, oceanic dead zones and islands of garbage, of seaboards swallowed by the brine; of worldwide intense weather, mass extinctions, ecological collapse. Imagined burning bodies inhabited yet by the essence, the spark; faces melting in death rain; crumbling buildings; steel structures being carried by bodies of lava; yards-wide, miles-long fissures opening across cities and houses and flailing figures falling into them.

All on a dissolvable, transitory world, a heaven, hell, special for each. On the rotating blue planet veiled in wispy white favored by fortune to be habitable that he was living on, where he wailed, whined, drank wine. Dreamt, desired, fornicated. Lost himself internally. In paranoia, fantasy, extreme self-involvement, indolence, intoxication, delusion, in listening to a highly critical and misguiding little voice; lost

30

himself in depression, to feeling like the zombie of a person prematurely and inhumanely murdered; and also in escapism, in exactly the kind of lunacy manufactured for the masses, a kind that was contagious, of which everywhere were traces.

———◦((•))◦———

He saw the deterioration of supermarkets; of discount clothing, 99-cent, convenience stores (slowly, one burned-out letter in the lit company logo at a time; their stucco walls cracking over years, over the course of three-hundred-six-ty-five-day increments; moss starting up from their foundations, just as nearby moss was growing through sidewalk fissures along with weeds and parched grass, just as grass was overtaking ruptured concrete that not much earlier had been a department store parking lot). Saw rusting steel shells sheltering mutilated pay phones, rat-bait on spring-loaded deathtraps in dusty corners; heard pleading voices of oppressed souls, contagion within them; thought: one was reared to be of rat-maze poison.

He recollected for some reason a viewcube jingle that had lain hidden in his subconscious; it was from a half-hour horror-comedy he had years ago sometimes watched:

Folks are going to die from strangulation, by steely, lethal hands—cold grip around their necks! Hey Chicago area! Here's Farns. Cold-grip serial killer. Cold grip on reality.

31

He watched the irreversible demise of a youthful dream. There would never again be a significant other, he wouldn't even want one; he'd generally stop wanting at all, have no or few friends, for decades live a dull routine; never would he have more than a little success or money. Helpless, he would watch it burn and over many hundreds of days watch the embers smolder, finally being carried away very slowly, wind-borne particles, until eventually not even ashes remained; and the newly denuded spot where these remains had been was his life, still he was alive; and after it was over he was happy, beyond accepting of, happy about its destruction by conflagration. He viewed his ruin as the prerequisite for another, far stronger version of himself to be born into the emptiness, the chaos and cruelty. A less needy, less naïve, less human him. A version automatonic, more difficult to destroy. An iteration that was better-informed, achievement-driven, even psychopathic.

The mountains, blue-gray above the haze, he, Mister Anonymous, had a window-view of became abstract; they were worthwhile and inaccessible, aesthetically pleasing and otherworldly. Life on Earth seemed to him akin to life in some kind of weird prison—and maybe all housed in it were being punished, punished for doings they did not remember.

Hours were spent in darkness. Thoughts thereof were bred. There was much weeping...

He felt like a guardian of souls; no, of just his own; of himself he asked, how is the job I'm doing?

It was a wide cell that could become hell, that led to a lot of derangement. It was his home—to his knowledge a home he had never asked to live in—and he, an occupant as insignificant as any in its existence, was conceivably, as many an other, deranged; an ill, doleful inmate whose exits perhaps numbered only one.

————))(((((((((((————

Wills broke or wills willed. Struggles were had, power lost or gained. There was a sort of beauty in strife, in human drama, superior to fiction. So many did damage to many they knew or interacted with for no reason save their ignorance. Wills were brains thought the observer, the reject, brains given bodies to perform actions. Some had been programmed to believe if they secreted an explosives belt under their coverings then walked into where infidels congregated and detonated they would awake to virgins, three score and a dozen, in the afterlife.

————))(((((((((((————

Magic on an aging-wheel! He didn't generally trust people in close proximity to the aging-wheel to which he was secured, his fellow citizens; they seemed mostly under- or incorrectly developed.

Like moss upon tree trunks that grows to die, he said to himself, lay down and experience the price.

Peace, finally, was desired; but the world of cracked gray streets under gray precipitating skies, litter everywhere and spitting gangstas walking with crooked caps and legs widespread to keep their pants from falling all the way down, people always engaged in their tech gadget, people yelling "Suck my asshole, bitch" from passing cars, and so many passing plague-like autos (the nihilistic world of people removed from reality and treating each other badly), was intensifying and felt like it would go on endlessly, and it all seemed symptomatic of the same disease—the disease of the world, which afflicted the mind (and the origin of which was the mind). And peace was always more precious and fleeting; and the crowded, mistreated, vindictive planet, as its human inhabitants devolved, was always more crowded, crueler, more resource-depleted—till the sane and good, people of intellect and tenacity, abandoned all hope but to disappear.

<hr>

He saw a stream of...tire shops and Chinese buffet and Vietnamese restaurants and donut shops and fast food businesses; saw, as shuffling shadows, 7-Elevens and Circle Ks, gas stations, liquor stores, tittie bars, chain coffeehouses, Wal-Marts and K-Marts and Home and Office Depots; an assortment of nonresidential multilevel edifices and office buildings; buildings, single-story, that were or seemed gray on lots that were gray. Saw, on a bright April late afternoon—on both sides of throbbing traffic lanes, two north, two south (shimmer of sun off rushing steel)—a river, seemingly unending, of the insipid commercial architecture of early 21st century America.

—————»«(•)»«—————

He was, he was thinking, a dual person, contradiction, of two sides either of which was exerting primary influence at a given time but both of which seemed ever simultaneously extant. A person of spiritual positives and negatives, in whom the negatives had grown a stronger force. Who had the misfortune to love while being unlovable, to want what he might but taste, or not even that—perhaps taste only visually/mentally.

So such a one delved, not totally consciously, more toward another side. A side of lightlessness; a side better not turned to, tuned into; an unfortunate side, that a mature spirit (in a place of maturity in a lifetime) would avoid or reject; a side, a pole, of deathliness that a spirit in transition might not apprehend.

The licentious, predatory, beastly side. Of the jackal, wolf, primeval, archetypal. Those that slept the same as but below the masses that slumbered while awake, harmonized with others living ant-existences, resided within comfortable domiciles furnished and adorned, traveled in chrome and plastic machines, and shunned, indirectly killed or longed to kill (maybe unknowingly) the "ill," the "wicked"—empty, self-serving terms employed to categorize such a type by the ebbing, flowing herds of dying, lying-to-themselves also-beasts; lemming-people who were also sick, whose minds were small or deluded, whose spirits did the word a disservice.

⸺⸺ ((◉)) ⸺⸺

Magic Mountain in Northern California—its greeting high, brightly colored twists of snake, its many roller coasters—was where he found himself one sunny day well into the aughts. "I hope you die" uttered a child below him, seven or eight, of Asian ancestry, who was looking up at people standing on the spiral staircase that was the last bit of the long line the boy stood near the start of. Sounds fine, thought Henry, but the odds are against it.

In a few minutes he was locked into a section of the the many-segmented train that would be propelled with velocity along a curling serpent of painted steel, a big yellow U across his upper body, legs dangling beside his girlfriend's; the cars jerked slowly forward and up. Near the exit, the ride having given him an externally suppressed rush, there were contemptuous- and sullen-looking faces of what for some reason appeared to be exclusively Asians and Hispanics standing in a jumble on a chain-link-bounded walkway as if locked in a crowded pin. Throughout the park were hypersexualized teenage girls, teenagers of big muscles and big asses nearly humping, ethnically Asian young women with visages of borderline irritation who resembled or were porn stars.

He remembered...how he used to find himself paralyzed in bed as a kid after waking in terror of unknown cause; and he would be rendered temporarily mute, his attempts at screams almost soundless. How there were people who had seen shadow people outside at night or caught them standing in corners of lit rooms, moving fluidly through dens; beings of objectives, of such origin as one only could speculate about, encounters with which sounded especially frightening.

An eighties-era *Sunset* magazine liquor ad in which, claimed his parents, the attuned and studious could discern what appeared to be a spirit lurking in smoke curling from a slender cigarette in a holder between the fingers of a big-haired model.

In another glossy magazine ad an out-of-place mist mysterious and red, low in the photo. A story involving levitating occultists who involuntarily transformed into beasts and, unable to remain recumbent on air, fell six feet, each landing on four paws.

Maggots appeared on the ceiling, wiggling inperceivably, some of them burrowing into its unexplainably moist, soft plaster, from which they had perhaps originated.

Vomit rotted in a plastic bag in a garbage receptacle of green plastic thicker and more durable, stained and germ-coated inanimate symbol of the horror of filth, waste; modernity. Of an era in which corporations were more prevalent and powerful, the government more involved; in which citizens were more physically modified, toxified; the public mind, the economy, more manipulated. A time and place of concrete or steel rectangular buildings tall, wide and widespread; everywhere cities packed with people, cars, commercial property—streets, highways, telephone and railroad lines crisscrossing them; radio towers, cell phone towers on the outer reaches of them; everywhere houses, lights, signs, lines, reflectors. Of pollution, poverty, overpopulation; an era in which the Earth and people were to power secondary to commerce, as they were to the master plans of the masters, bad for the bulk of people. In which individuals could be said to truly own little. A place, a time of: the internet, unlimited free pornography, social networking websites, dating sites; omnipresent gadgets, media overload. In which one kind of zombie was obsessed with another and many lives were wasted looking at screens; the culture of a mean, arrogant society (with a death wish) was vacuous, debased (everyone getting to live a life of ease unharassed by big brother for as long as they shut up and, ideally, if aware of it, accepted their relative powerlessness (at least until they were part of a better-armed majority)—the subjects of the State grateful for the perks provided them by the godlike government that kept them).

Once upon a time, in a city of the extreme southwestern United States... There was an old lean homeless black man who purported to know the future. Encountering him on a sidewalk in a humid ghetto one night Henry stopped and let himself be briefly talked at, mildly curious. He didn't remember much of what he said, but most of it was pretty general. It seemed to Henry—yet young, approachable—he'd come across a few of them.

On the edge of the walkway were a number of grocery carts of the vagabond's, neatly filled with all the owner's worldly possessions, the remainder of such a person's possessions mostly without value even sentimental. There were some shiny trinkets, a piece of mirror, moldy toys, scratched photographs of strangers joined and bordered with duct tape, a hotplate, a water-damaged journal filled with symbols and illegible cursive in ink, cheap framed icons—a haloed Mary, blood-dripping Jesus. Torn tee-shirts in need of laundering hung over the metal edges of the carts that, other than his person, held everything he had accumulated and at present managed to hold onto, empty cans, boxes of Glad bags filling their lower levels.

Wiry, maybe sixty, thereabouts, he was like a suddenly materializing sage who, late in the evening, had appeared on a desolate street surrounded by rundown buildings, in a conversant mood.

He said things that many did, talked of things that according to one theory would happen only because the collective unconscious caused them to, talked in archetypes: the evil leader would come, the Antichrist, the great era of tribulation they were already living during.

He once dreamt (had it been a dream?) of a man in the basket of a hydraulic crane being electrocuted while working on a transformer (it was terribly loud, the boom the instant he was killed— and horrific, especially to a young child. Though happening in a split second it had been so realistic as to at once become permanently singed in his mind), and falling, scorched—with a thud he might not have heard (maybe because he woke immediately in voiceless sweating terror)—to the ground.

(He'd dreamt once too as a boy (it was a dream, alarmingly palpable, which woke him similarly—but then he'd been able to half-scream) of sitting with his parents at the circus at about seven when suddenly one of the huge wood beams that supported the big top came crashing down directly on a child seated behind him and to his right, certainly causing the similarly aged boy's death. ...Or had it been a real event?)

As a child, he seemed to remember, he had had an uneasiness about such cranes (which may have been because of the dream or event involving one or may have preceded it), and he used to have a fear related to the fire trucks that were among those vehicles to which they were attached; he thought he might once have witnessed something tragic, traumatizing just across the street from his longtime family home, across the medium-sized often-parched yard, that involved the two (a fireman weighed down by protective yellow, helmet with shield, boots, hose who'd been lifted to a second-story window from which fire licked and poison smoke gushed, debris-cloud gray, among unruly orange, who was overcome by smoke)—but he couldn't place any such memory, and it probably wasn't true. He'd had a fear then also of anyone in a mask, the more so the more face-obscuring, protuberant, alien, and especially if it was attached to a back-strapped oxygen tank or two; there was a mysteriousness, ominousness, about such things that, streamed through a mind early in development, turned them terrifying.

Henry imagined the morbidest possibilities when he remembered past fear-invoking situations, and at times other. He had a morbid side, an interest in destruction (a natural curiosity if about nothing else the finality of the animal body) and decadence, in the depraved, the bestial, the unnatural, aberrant, fortunately rare, e.g. awful deformities and heinous homicides, and in his teen years especially would often nourish it with desensitizing images, videos—many of the multitude that occupied open cyberspace. With macabre, perhaps esoteric, history; with porn, accident photos, ruins humanus.

Always he had himself run a bit toward the aberrant, the dark. As a kid he had for his age been particularly sexual, psychologically. His fantasies—though it was maybe not unusual—had included grown women from about the time he was eight years old, and at around eleven, twelve he from time to time fantasized about the young wife (thirtyish) of an authority figure in his life, fantasies that cast her as a lace-clad teacher figure (in which, rather than engage in sexual acts he was not yet aware of, she mainly leaned on him, sat in his lap, while kissing him; feeding him, in a sexual manner).

41

One afternoon in Brooklyn he was a bit drunk or stoned and feeling carefree, feeling happy actually, and was standing with his seemingly similarly feeling roommate on the roof of their building (they had never been up there and the door wasn't locked) and without a thought (in part because of how carefree he felt) he threw over the edge, onto the street, two heavy, basically full, buckets of tar that were up there—sunbaked, metal-handled—which might have resulted in vehicular damage or even manslaughter. ("Why did you do that?" his lady friend had asked, serious, on reentering with him the small apartment on the third floor, 3B, in which they shared a makeshift bedroom. And he had not known the answer.) The next day there was a high pile of tar on the sidewalk in front of the building and two black-uniformed cops cuts close-cropped knocked on the door who were questioning people in each unit and spoke briefly to Henry and his friend, both of whom were convincing in their obliviousness.

He remembered...a man with a broken foot who, as he went slowly along, was whining an inauthentic, tragicomic whine. Homeless in appearance, African ethnically, he wore soiled orange warmups with double white stripes down the sides, had a yellow-dyed mohawk, and was traversing downtown in the hardening snow, in the slush and ice, on crutches—all the time exaggeratedly fake-whining.

Around cold, dead brown eyes were whites of yellow. He seemed deranged but was hardly unkempt, seemed vacant but not resigned.

He seemed to mock the inferior imagined sorrows of all without looking at anyone, and no one dared look upon him. One who was observing him speculated that the broken foot was the result of deserved violence or a just mishap; for some reason felt the most compassionate thing to do for him was to summarily execute him, as one would a rabid dog. Or instead to off oneself, in order to exit a world of such sights of low-level though evident horror—impossible to bring oneself to view but from across a chasm psychological.

———— ((●)) ————

There was heat in the lock of two organisms of the same species and opposite sexes; in bodies coitally twined, the connection of two variations on one design, warmth was multiplied by warmth.

There was a moment when muscles became taut, the organ within a woman's body was most engorged; when time seemed to stop, just before the release; and as it happened there was the primal scream of humanity being born, the image of the upper half of a Neolithic person lifting itself from a pool of primordial sludge in a clearing in woods over the undergrowth of which green fog crept.

There was a pulling, the instinct of creation, survival, the take-over of the animal; there was something awry, a feeling

43

of ownership, a brutality in the yearning of the mechanism to force inward, deeper, to drive toward the womb, to excrete in the throes, the paralysis of climax—leaving the other a used receptacle, stimuli-provider, leaking byproduct; even before ejaculation was over there was a vacuousness.

Then sadness, pickling quickly to regret, longing (but for what was not known)—the affectionless duty done, the machine idle, its sole objective achieved, the mindless fucking of a pair of dumb animals at an end (codes for additional such dumb animals, another thousand, million, milliard, in the female's cavities, in and around a ruby-red mouth turned sex hole, absorbed by bodily orifices, consumed for pay by the organism bright-lit and brightly made up in now-smeared thick makeup, destroyed by the acid in the stomach of a public prostitute).

Sadness second, first a perceivable vacuum, a black hole—the viscous coital seal uncomfortably broken, breasts splattered; the warmth of forever having flashed across the woman's eyes, deep-brown distant void-eyes, her face, as the blankness lifted from it (she having liked it in a way, being splashed with life, teeming biological goo, that of a stranger, in a video-moment of her moon face, a ruin of testosterone; particular tactile and nonphysical sensations, tastes, new and intense in her memory).

Circuitous motion, degradation, desolation.

———— ((◦)) ————

No one enjoyed their life, practically no one. Few were

44

happy; yet the standard was more or less frequent doses of happiness, which was overrated anyway. Said Schopenhauer life was a condition to be endured. Everyone was waiting, rotting, for a future time of completeness, lasting fulfillment, that would never come.

———————— ((◐)) ————————

Inside he pretended, tried to convince himself that there weren't times he thought about, say, ripping someone nearly in half with a scimitar or digging his fingers, joyously, exploratively, into the gore of the freshly deceased.

Maybe throwing some around, examining gristle, spitting into hollow eye sockets...maybe while a crowd (of dream-figures meant therefore only as non-interfering extras) was watching, aghast, having formed an circle around the homicide perpetrator and victim—a jaggedly broken major bone, a ruin of femur in a devastation of (now released) asleep sheep that had once and for too long bleated obnoxiously, jutting from discolored skin and fatty pink-red flesh.

———————— ((◐)) ————————

He had experienced sometimes, for periods, the sensation of everything being dead, or concealed, or lies; faded, forgotten (or never known). He worried sometimes that he would never be satisfied with a single permanent sexual partner (because the most desirable, sexually, to him would want nothing of him, or he was not normal enough for a mating of durability, did not sufficiently mesh with anyone, was not a viable candidate for acceptance; however, as others, could be used, wondered about, lusted for, forgotten about); on occasion he worried he'd spend the remainder of his physically functional days overly poor, at a job he (at best) didn't much like (and that definitely didn't offer much in the way of raises, benefits, upward mobility), the kind of job that quickly caused one to become burnt out, that could make the best-adjusted person a bit crazy.

—((●))—

Sometimes, in dreams, dreams always too brief and so the sweeter...he inhabited a clean, comfortably furnished house also populated by two beautiful young women—women who adored him, whom he was as close to as anyone could be to anyone. And the house and he and they were all that existed in the world, and he had nothing to do but enjoy existence, be happy, in a state of worrilessness, with two lover-companions. They lived there, without want, in a house huge and lovely, always warm, that existed in a dimension in which they did not age.

He dreamt on occasion there was a woman in his life, a blonde perhaps slightly his junior, who was his soulmatch lover and image of perfection, and they too spent their time, timeless time, in a state of pure affection and utter happiness, total love, a love that was allowed to exist outside of real-world concerns and complications, outside of aging;

they were no age particularly, what looked the equivalent of youngish adult, and stayed that way. They never felt hunger, but they ate, for enjoyment, to savor delicious food; often they feasted on one another's lips, he on her neck and bosom and the drunk-making perfume that emanated from these.

Dreamt once—no, it had happened—that a fiftyish guy (a white guy, his showing skin dirt-coated, his eyes shifty), everything dark about him, brown, organic, his very proximity unease-causing, sat himself across from Henry at a bar and soon offered him some mushrooms he had in a piece of brown recycled-paper grocery bag that he untied, placing them on the table. He imagined later the horrible trip and agonizing liver failure death that probably would have resulted from consumption of the brown medium-size fungi bundled in the paper and felt then spite for the stranger with the strange manner and suspicious package, who was perhaps evil.

<hr/>

All was real but also unreal, because truly it was all the equivalent of a dream that was not recognized as such, everyone just taking a voyage (more often unpleasant than pleasant, at least in memory) through collective reality, the collective universe, the matrix where dreams were played out—Earth the part of the matrix where so-situated souls (which were all one, all souls being ultimately fragments of the same mind) were having all of their mortal experience one tiny fraction of eternity at a time (fractions of the boundless of course not

47

actually being possible), a dreamworld in a larger world of dreamworlds replete with fantastic dream-creatures having fanciful and horrific day-imaginings, and closest to free of their putrefying carcasses when dreaming within the dream.

———•((•))•———

He saw a youngish man's teeth and overall face destroyed, saw him otherwise bodily fucked up (and saw him freak out during his vicious beating) by random thug types, without prior provocation or communication, one late evening, the sky starless. On the asphalt before him the man saw pieces of his front teeth, saw his dirty, bloody hand—a hand shiny with the stuff under the moon, dark coagulating red. Fear, hate, destruction, chaos in urban perdition...

The apartment of a solitary, sad man in his early thirties: an apartment of white walls almost bare, in which was a refrigerator with around a score of magnetic letters on its front, two pages featuring nude women ripped from a men's magazine taped on one side (a blonde, a brunette below her); a computer (not expensive or new) in one corner of the living room (on a desk faced by a simple wooden chair with a blue-upholstered back), a living room containing two sofas (one cushioned, the other not), an oblong Formica-topped coffee table between them; above this, on the ceiling, formed by hundreds of beer bottle caps, a star, with a scar (a sort of vein in one point where the caps wouldn't stay in the ceiling because of its texture)...

The day after being fired another in a string of irate postal workers, this one in his early sixties, retaliated, showing up at the post office he'd worked in with two five-gallon buckets filled with a mixture of porcupine ordure and worms that he splashed numerous of his recent coworkers with...

An adaptive mass killer and misogynist had a ball (was the belle of the ball) in penitentiary by means of estrogen augmentation and a muscular ethnically African boyfriend. By the time a documentary crew checked in on him where he had been incarcerated for decades for his heinous act more of his adulthood than not had been spent snorting coke, becoming feminine, and sucking dick in a generally unpleasant, seemingly timeless hole (among the inhabitants of which the law as much as anywhere was that of the jungle). The murderer was a man-woman in his middle forties whose brain and body chemistry were all askew, who would probably die into the same bleakness...

He realized belatedly the general wrongness of antisocietal behavior (such as random violence; concern only for oneself, one's own feelings), some of the roots of which he understood through internal experience.

Henry, Orlan saw, as he'd earlier seen in himself the worst, was, had been the definition of a young man

49

benighted—dwelling in ignorance, overcome by darkness.

Orlan, via Henry, realized that he had long been a puny entity, foolish among many alike (realized that he, a man older than Henry, modern, was ignorant, all too ignorant, and for too long had so remained—until his experience in Oxon); that he had often been wrong or misguided; was intentionally or unintentionally tragic, self-defeating; incredibly imperfect and in many or most ways quite ordinary.

He planned to strive—he would strive henceforth, with the entirety of his new knowledge (finally, difficultly attained, its truth evident), toward greater awareness, self-knowledge; toward a knowledge of love, toward knowing the enjoyment of just being extent, being a marvelous essence in a shell on an interstellar spinning sphere.

Nietzsche wrote, he recalled, only by being could joy be assured, that change and joy could not coexist; that the most enlightened want was to join with what was rather than what was undergoing alteration.

Orlan thought back to discovering the fortress (snow was melting, becoming grayish slush on a knobby far-stretching field of green. It was cold, very cold, but not unbearably for someone wearing long-johns under their jeans and a leather jacket—like the battered black one Orlan wore over a white tee.

Functionally dressed Orlan—who, like most men of his era, was a cruel, somewhat exaggeratedly masculine survivalist who usually had a five o'clock shadow and the fixed grimace of a headache (his face rough, wide, ruddy; topped by trimmed, wavy, sable hair going white around the forehead, a forehead of earned lines)—was thinking about the emptiness of the surroundings in the crisp winter air. About the impressive fortification before him: solitary in the wilderness; immune-, indifferent-, impregnable-looking; somehow intimidatingly ridiculing, its might (the fact of its presence, surrounded by nature) antagonizing; seeming to tell quietly, in a whisper wordless, of secret knowledge in impenetrable passages that descended and kept on to depths unfathomable, locations unmerciful.

He was directly outside it, where it indented the land, and it was thirty or more feet tall; and for a half-moment the titanium-looking mass seemed to flicker, its whole image, the totality of the incongruent structure. And—disoriented, the bitter weather getting to him, with no memory of how he had come to occupy the expanse of frozen grass, of the last hours or days—he sought entry to it. And looming over him was the need to place himself, an unfamiliar unease).

Thought back to when in the brightness within he met Keen, Lark (her apparent junior) and the other thin white gown-garbed humans or humanoids (were they even humanoid—shapeshifters maybe?) inhabiting the odd structure. To when in testing Keen's explanation of the place he'd imagined into being, or Oxon had imagined for him,

51

the gleaming staircase he'd journeyed up—farther into his imagination (or Oxon's?)—and never come down. Or had he? What the fuck is going on? he thought he said aloud but didn't hear himself. What the fuck was going on...today?

Today. Was it still the same day? Had more than twenty-four hours passed? Was there still time? Was there still matter? Was he physically extent?

If so, where am I...what is I? he was thinking, in a white void, apparently bodiless. *A thought. Consciousness.*

⸺⸻◦《◉》◦⸻⸺

Some people, it seemed to Orlan, were created for destruction, early or relatively unnaturally—this, ruin, finding its way to them ineluctably, often circuitously, by degrees. Souls unfortunate, prone to misfortune, or who made their own misfortune—who were never sufficiently conscious to free themselves from miseries unnecessary.

⸺⸻◦《◉》◦⸻⸺

Earth was a laboratory for souls. They were there exposed to certain conditions, processes, for a definite and finite period unknown to them. None of the journey could be said to be predetermined however; if the future could be seen one nonetheless had their will. What would happen would happen, in the big menagerie—where the greatest show on the planet cerulean was always everywhere ongoing.

52

Once glimpsed, in a silver top stretched by her sizable bust, in a supermarket bustling on a Monday in the early evening, was a young woman of perceived sexual perfection, of much value as material when less than a half-hour later while remembering, picturing her as vividly as possible he powerfully climaxed—magnificent beast thinking of magnificent beast. Crazy beast among crazy beasts; among hollow beasts, beasts always in reflection; beasts with more hair and less, who were more or less sebaceous, who possessed appeal more broad or less. Beasts of the spinning blue world. Beasts of various ages (degrees of maturation, desiccation, deterioration) and forms, of various mental and bodily capacities, beasts reared in myriad circumstances, born all into the same unknownness, equally amnesiac. Beasts of two extremes, two poles, poles that could be called (and always were simplistically called some variation of) good and bad.

There were, everywhere, so many who were so damaged; so tragically unknowing, hateful; hateful often unconsciously, and ignorant (by definition) always so.

So many who were materially rich and spiritually lacking spent so much of their time thinking they were exceedingly special, human paragons. Went about thinking of their being thought about, looked at, lusted for—sometimes because they were lonesome, sometimes because they were vain, often the two.

They wanted to be important (believe they were in a way that, deep, they didn't), intriguing, desired; all of them thought of themselves as, to all appearances, attractive packages. They knew many people locally and their primary needs were met—except an internal one so important that they shut it out. Its voice, maybe soft and heard infrequently, perhaps loud and talkative, did not fit with how they'd tried to fashion and how they regarded themselves, their manufactured identity and its assorted accouterments, all that their (overlarge) egos clung to. It was something like a basic, innocent, helpless longing. It seemed of an earlier time, had been rejected long ago by felt necessity in order to self-preserve, and had the power to bring tears. It even seemed related to a part of them that was able to be pleased by a passing butterfly, a row of tulips, watching a squirrel; to feel connection in flash eye contact with a stranger.

———————————⟨◉⟩———————————

He thought of the millions of desirable women he'd never have sexual congress with; thought of legs shapely and smooth, skirts short and jeans tight, breasts high and firm; thought he perhaps lusted more intensely for the animate object the less he felt there a chance of possessing it (the delectable piece of meat), however briefly.

The blue world rotated, undergoing a slow steady sweet soft subtle symphony of deterioration, people and the creations of people becoming dilapidated. Pillars crumbled, fell in white dust explosions; stucco cracked and buildings molted and molded; sentimental items, dust-filmed decades-old mementos, molecularly faded from one temporal state to become, gradually, trivially, part of other fleeting configurations as insubstantial as any—unless animate objects, like organisms that think, play, feel complex pain (until reconfiguration, when they become memories, particles, maybe ideas—they bred of the strangeness, silliness, wonder (possibility; inevitability; elements, stardust); those who were of it, the diverse cluster spinning in the vacuum; those who were, for a cosmic split second. Those part of the organism that was one, with many minds and energies, a heterogeneous conglomeration dwelling on another organism, one naturally just right climatologically. A single organism of multifarious heads, skins, shapes, that had long had a beneficial relationship with a gyrating living ball of rock, water-topped, isolated due to its inhabitants' early-stage evolution from others inhabited and habitable spread among the stars (in the infinite sea of highly pressurized nothing)—a ball the organism was forcing to destroy it, annihilation growing stronger in its collective psyche).

Physical death was not the death of consciousness...but wary was he of the psychological experience of having a mutilated or ruined body, that unpurchased suit that kept one attached to the spinning fire-filled organismal sphere that was for some and at times, such times as when one was painfully destroying oneself (corporeally) with immediacy seen and felt, the hellacious setting of ineffable reality, which one could only hope not was primary reality but only a bizarre situation, a playing out of variables, symphonic play of lifeforms diverse in an atmosphere perfect for their growth—sprinkled somewhere in the void, another point of light in a whirlpool of such phenomena, objects that were for humankind immensities, randomly situated in the largest of immensities.

He found laughable the illusions of society, people's so-called desires, supposed values; the belief in an invisible patriarchal judge, loveless unions that should never have been, the accumulation of things, the production of nasty replacements who would be far nastier than their progenitors by midlife. Who wanted to be tied down to a monotonous job they disliked that had nothing to do with their interests and to a middleaged wrinkling blob of personness, unmindful children always running about? (Probably no life was as good as it might sound however, and if love was real it could almost certainly be found with a sexually unideal person. And life was a learning experience, one that if possible was to be endured, nothing more; it could be heaven and hell.)

On television ubiquitous much of the programming was not worth the time; yet there were those who spent most of their waking hours zoned out in front of one (or/and eating), soaking up radiation and numbing themselves intellectually. Watching—or hypnotized by (not only by the animal-brain-piquing fare but by the glow, the low hum, of the brainwave-altering apparatus)—soap operas, of all sorts; absurd talk shows; all manner of "reality" shows that among a wealth of bad were terrible; police state propaganda of the hour-long scripted drama variety; entertainment shows primarily about the famous and often obnoxious, many of them reality TV stars, some of them vacated societally-superior shells of people; commercials for new movies, new vehicles, fast food, feminine hygiene products; ads for side-effect-ridden pharmaceuticals that the faceless with and without various afflictions were told by makeup-caked averagely attractive actors at various stages of adulthood to ask their physician about. Advertisements in which former film stars, senior citizens, recommended brands of diapers, dietary supplement brands, life insurance companies for those in their second childhoods; commercials for baby wipes, frosted cereal, pressurized cheese. Ads such as one for artificial juice that featured digital English-speaking anthropomorphic animals; or one for a company that prominently promoted the popular frozen dairy product it manufactured in innovative voluminous varieties starring a character with an upturned waffle cone for a head, pink ice cream shoulders—the corporation's unnaturally chipper mascot. Or those for a national burger chain the face of which was a urbane, deep-voiced, tie-and-tails-clothed, white-haired of-course-English butler who always lifted the lid from a tray he held to reveal a tall, steaming professed example of the company's newest burger—which, while similar to the ones the hoary, wizened woman and brown boy consumed happily in the bright clean lobby in the commercials, in reality was without exception unhealthy-tasting, less pleasing to the eye and less substantial; and the girl or guy who handed it to one never seemed to be as good-looking, cheery or dentally perfect as those in the viewcube spots; and in real life when one sat in the lobby they were made nauseous to see the man who sat at the table in front of them eat, and accidentally put their elbow in some diced onions on their table that they hadn't noticed; and felt lethargic after their meal, had a stomachache later, maybe had even been poisoned.

<hr />

America was a cruel homeland; dangerous (though it was possible for it to become, it had previously been, more so), shallow-peopled, totalitarian, jingoistic, out for itself—a corporatocracy, ultimately financier-owned and -run. The old dream was dead (new and other dreams went on) but some still delusionally clung to what had long been a lie. And in this cold realm of myths recent and not, this partly pulchritudinous ever being made uglier land, lived another sad, mad creature of self-confusion (who was he? an adapted machine? a highly complex computer that changed at a level below awareness with the influx of input?), its animal reactions repressed and disguised. It had lost so much; it lost itself. Its true self had been forgotten and/or never fully developed, only the false self—an adaptation/maladaptation— was allowed (by itself ultimately) to survive. Or did the real self lie in hiding deep and mostly undetectable, still hating what it hated, liking what it liked, all the more so because of its being forcibly hidden or mutated? What did it do to the soul, such measures? Cause derangement?

Sometimes he wasn't present or at least was not externally engaged; he'd once felt permanently gone spiritually and emotionally (though able to meagerly imitate pleasant emotions, and (likely) capable of easily accessing negative ones). An unwanted cloak of depression would fall over him, for reasons not so strange; illusion, nightmare make their mark on reality—animal-life dumb-reality (so often lonely, so ultimately) on the planet chill and gray (ever-altering like bodies) despite its sunsets, flora, too-infrequent scapes of beauty. (Planet strewn with transparent plastic receptacles. Of establishments where employees who displayed their tits for tips served frothy poison and one maybe spoke for the only time to poisoned strangers who were sometimes red-faced and sweaty, oftentimes addicted—places in which a patron might lean against the bar, a brisk illogical stream of thoughts flowing through his brain, the way his eyes look making him appear as abstracted as he is, drinking to murder memory cells, to quiet the water.)

⸺◉⸺

The tall tale of 3/27 worked because everyone saw it on TV, presented as nonfiction, presented via supposedly live news feeds from the supposedly always trustworthy five big networks (allegedly five different feeds); the plants on the streets and reporters told the public what they were to be told, and of course the country's leaders all at once played indignant, it was time for retribution (by means of invading a dirt-poor country the so-called perpetrators didn't even hail from). And the country's populace, a minority of whom were smart enough even to question the story after, or ever, as desired immediately saw red, and those here and there who had the perspicacity and moxie to have doubts about what was fed them—"It was on TV, plenty of people saw the planes" (plenty of people, on TV, *said* they saw the planes, primarily people working for one of the five aforementioned media outlets) responded the plebeians—were treated the same as or worse than commies or commie sympathizers in the country in the fifties. But the same mass of evidence the majority of the nation said proved the veracity of the undebatable official scenario was the same evidence that still existed to prove something much different entirely, something the implications of which were worse than U.S. and other government action "in response" to the acts supposedly executed by Islamic extremists, the increase in terrorism against the West, the physical and psychological effect on populaces.

March twenty-seventh was a classic psych op (again): the big five news channels' feeds were controlled from one location (the competing stations often used the same shot, with different tones and additions), the footage they aired not quite live and doctored in ways such as to include cartoon (poor-quality CGI) planes—the "aircraft" said to have caused the free-fall collapse of the towers, which was in actuality the result of controlled demolition using weapons-grade thermite. It was televised deception—like the application of a false flag operation to accomplish major goals not without precedent in American history—and it was a poetic deception, bringing down national monuments in the geographic heart of capitalist avarice as a means to erode civil liberties further and faster; to wage wars (that were part of a larger endless war, against a nationless enemy, an idea, a seed planted by the bellicose and that seed's fruit—directed violence) of much collateral damage against distant supposed foes (strategically or otherwise beneficial wars against less-funded created adversaries). It was a covert, a midnight-black operation because of which xenophobia was nurtured, a false paradigm fostered, and existence ended early for certain Middle Easterners and Westerners, in many cases believers in two different gods of Abraham, the former of whom happened to live in nations the invaders considered lucrative or important objectively, who by and large were disparate from their land's occupiers, had much different perspectives, lived more simply, naturally—hadn't had baby fat since being babies. The public of the major invading country ought to have

61

been enraged about the nation's socioeconomic problems, the prioritization of ruinous military campaigns, the many big deceits—deceits that led to platoons of young adult fodder being shipped to forbidding foreign lands. But they couldn't be expected to if they didn't know the half of the lies, if they were (on a case-by-case basis willfully) blind—and if they were it abetted their masters, abusers domestically and abroad.

Daily increasing was the number of unjustifiable American and a great many Afghan and Iraqi casualties, and the price tag for unjust wars to propel an agenda that hurt many more; in fact most of the world populace had been adversely affected by the actually long-ongoing global war against people, the lock-down (of which, for instance, the illegality of marijuana was a small part)—for that was what was and had been afoot: a Global War on People—based on cunning plans that involved fabrication, wrongful death, high treason. Most recently the successful fiction that was 3/27 (the original story still the one being run), the fiction that got the imperial powers' flocks to head down exactly the dark tunnel the handful of malevolent sheepherders intended them to.

<hr />

He saw a man who at twenty-five, after a counseling session at a community mental health clinic—due to parts of what he divulged that couldn't legally be kept secret (that he felt both homicidal and suicidal)—became a ward of the state. In the mostly bare, small, unpersonalized and foreign-feeling apartment he was relegated to soon thereafter he was recorded in every room, the tininess, worthlessness his life had been unfairly reduced to subject to strict, thoroughly enforced rules. What he read was selected by his keepers, smileless state employees; what he wrote and didn't destroy was read by them. What he'd written that wasn't approved was taken, never to be returned—all part of therapy, the healing process they said—and all such material presumably went into his file. Confiscated pages—the person who came to his domicile and did the taking was the only agent of the agency he saw regularly, an expressionless, approximately middle-aged, medium-build woman, her brown hair consistently worn in a bun—were read by at least one employee of the department that oversaw him (he suspected it was her) and, he guessed, distributed to other parties, to characterless or clerical-looking people in other bureaucratic arms who read his mind's outpourings sometimes amused, sometimes bemused, sometimes disquieted (in small drab offices, at desks, in typically multilevel square buildings packed with such offices, premises of regional, state, and federal bureaus). It didn't stop him that they (always the same impersonal woman of the state, crisp, dressed like a half-century-old fossil, a psychiatrist who visited weekly, whom he of course disliked and thought he also would have under different circumstances) seized most of his outlet output; he wrote frenzily, more prodigiously than ever he had, the ideas he expressed more violent than they'd ever been, his stories more disturbing since their, her, first having seized them—partly because he knew they would be read by the judging strangers, *because*

63

what was stole if it was of any intrinsic value was as good as destroyed. But his life he felt, he knew, was over; there was no more little kernel of hope, everything he did and might do was futile except as a means of occupying himself (as days of a life turned tragedy continued uncounted, demarcated only by stretches of sleep during which he had oneiric experiences that caused him sadness or anxiety). And his head was a festering cancer on him, his unchecked mind given so little stimuli to distract and direct it. For he had just the walls to look at (a washed-out beige, unadorned), had some writing utensils and paper, and some magazines and books—about ten of each, among the latter *A Tree Grows in Brooklyn* and a volume of Heraclitus he ended up reading (the sight of the spine of which caused him to think involuntarily of the fact that "Heraclitus" contained the words "her" and "clit")— none of which he had or would have chosen.

———— ((◦)) ————

Orlan in Oxon was...a dream of form within a dream of form—forms, forms always metamorphosing, variegated forms of many artful designs, of various meanings and roles: a kaleidoscope like a photo show of Earth scenes pristine, as vivid as surroundings; as seemingly real as a woman passing on the sidewalk in the sunshine, on a sun-soaked day in June in the metropolis, a self-confident woman in maroon silk that seems a part of her perfect shape, above which is a most alluring visage topped by bouncing black hair shining in the daylight, a woman who seems to belong in the setting, who would perhaps seem to belong in any setting.

———•((•))•———

Lust for most was only experienced less frequently over time, the end of lust if not because of death occurring only if a specimen survived to senescence, typically advanced senescence, or its body or mind were transformed other than by old age in a way detrimental to carnality. But such drives, impulses, feelings made one human. Made one the sad, silly carnal beast, one face of the one human.

———•((•))•———

Human thought had always had the capacity to become insane, and historically often went in that direction; civilizations had typically or always been or degenerated to lunacy, as demonstrated again and again over centuries. Humans made robots, therefore the potentiality existed for their robots to become insane or be so produced, or to immediately or eventually take control, perhaps for their insane makers' own "good." But there were a lot of insane robots about already; anyway something close enough.

———•((•))•———

He saw edifices housing machinery of the State, the

façades of which featured stone-carved rapacious-looking demons; dragons with tails that ended in the shape of arrowheads...

On an American coast, egesta-coated clams. Shit and urine, their stench filling the surrounding air; soggy scraps of toilet paper in a brown sludge under an overcast sky, the result of a ruptured sewage pipe hidden near the occidental ocean, in beach sand, somewhere lapped occasionally by the sea, causing the filth to be carried into the brine. Littorals streaked with feces, others rimmed by petroleum; overly acidic oceans (dead in plenty of places) containing copious oil, plastic; beaches spotted with balls of toxic muck washed up on them, with marine animals suffering beneath oleaginous gunk...

———)((O))———

It was a sad fact, but typical of the human condition, particularly typical of a human being that was a Westerner, that so much of his life had now been spent nonbeneficially in the tragic, ongoing but ever escapable realm of mind and time (time delusive; like the mind, its critical little voice crazy-making and loquacious).

———)((O))———

One night in central China Henry went alone to an upscale restaurant, where he ordered the sweet and sour pork he had recently been craving, and where he ended up having a spontaneous (perhaps not his first but his worst) episode of obsessive-compulsive behavior. Again and again he folded his napkin; he wiped the table with it over and over, constantly, determined there should be no discernible specks or moisture (except the ring under his cold drink) anywhere on its surface; he was psychotically preoccupied with everything being arranged on the table in a specific way, in the one and only "correct" way. His boss, as fate would have it, showed up to dine there too that night, taking a table not far away, and in the midst of Henry's craziness came over to introduce him to *his* boss—to whom he undoubtedly gave the impression of being mentally ill—and the eye contact between Henry and his spectacled superior before the latter took leave of the table seemed to indicate something like one quarter contempt, a quarter disgust, one quarter disappointment, and a quarter confusion. And he felt a little sorry for him, a little regretful, and remained in the abnormal state that even then he believed he'd willed himself into (for some reason) and could control (but inexplicably was choosing not to).

Maybe, he speculated—later; possibly while he was still at the restaurant—his mysterious, likely voluntary behavior was due to general poor mental health, which at that point he was already sure he suffered from, its poorness then (due to whatever cause or causes) seemingly having reached a peak.

———◉———

Marijuana had long ago come to make him paranoid or

67

lethargic; he realized this but nevertheless still smoked regularly, partly because he felt it a necessity (in order to cope). Cigarettes, finally, had come to make him feel like death, but then so much else about his day-to-day life and mental condition made him if not feel like be reminded of death. As if that was somehow the theme of so much that constituted the strange life, here on Earth, that he'd come to feel was not the realer or real life (Earth, the physical world, he felt, was not the realm of truer, ultimate reality).

———◦⟪◉⟫◦———

Free will was a specter as terrifying as any; Oxon was or maybe was a version of his free will made manifest. It was not like a drug trip but a lot like a trance. A trance of mercurially changing people, happenings, locales...

One man had a dream, long-reoccurring, about surviving throat cancer, living the remainder of his days without a voice box. (Becoming a larynxless monster with a mechanical voice who lived another thirty, mostly isolated, years (who even if he might have spent time with his young grandchildren before he died would have scared them to tears). Years spent reflective, going always back in his mind through the past, unwillingly, years spent mainly in mental misery. Years that seemed long, nightmarish, but briefer than the previous score and a half.) A dream that led to his finally quitting smoking.

There was a wealth of despicableness in the history of the internecine species, reams and tomes of evil (and so far as American history went the dawn of the industrial age did not mark the commencement of a less nefarious era but if anything was the beginning of a time of greater evil, in which it had more avenues, sometimes convoluted). So much blood, injustice, so much of it ultimately because of avarice, due to reaching ever and anywhere for resources needed or felt to be or only coveted.

The civilization he saw was from the get-go a slow sure disaster; probably any city-state model would eventually become chaos, necrotize from the inside out, devolve into decadence—be a failure by design.

As the character said in the movie rant, it was like everything everywhere had gone crazy, as if everything had deteriorated or was deteriorating. Society was the sum of all its members and ubiquitous were those not even a little okay, not based on the prevailing societal standard—and far greater was the number of people who were quite distant from the mark judging by a standard of more import. Earth was the only Hell, though it didn't have to be, and the only one there ever had been.

"Answer me something," began the grizzled glinting-eyed

69

middleaged bristly bum to the non-bum of his species and sex he sat beside. "Would you become a prostitute in order to live comfortably?" His mouth hung a little open and eyes were the same as before as he looked still at the face of the younger man, whose countenance his words had altered. This man remained unspeaking and so the bum, who liked the change he'd produced and below his consciousness was invigorated by it, added, "It doesn't need an addendum, what I just said, but I hope the answer's 'no,' in your case or anyone's. I hope that people aren't so willing to be whores, to go against themselves in the worst way. I hope that people would rather undergo pain or death... But," he hung his head now a bit, "sadly, I'm afraid that with rare exceptions that isn't true." They sat on the perimeter of a park on a bench of green-painted iron, rivets, dry, knobby wood that was superficially identical to many others that circled the park, in the center of which was a playground where presently at midday two children the size of ants at the distance, similarly aged siblings of opposite genders, while casually watched by their pop novel-reading mother, were playing on and among the area's apparatuses—merry, sweaty, intense, immersed. "In a big way I really am afraid of that," he said after a moment. "Now." He cast a glance at the man half his age then looking back to a point across the park where nothing but grass was visible said, "You have to ask yourself what a prostitute is, other than someone who offers sexual favors for money; what sort of things would make *you* feel that way, I mean like a prostitute, outside of that."

Wonder and horror were likely in store for those who intentionally eyelid tripped with lights off, especially if they were stoned—a kaleidoscope of unpredictable images, sometimes quite frightening, clear (and often grotesque, such as perhaps grotesque faces, visages like gargoyles'); figures that came into focus as the images seemed to rush closer. It was like being in a centrifuge of mind pictures (and one after another a picture became discernible). A place that was no place, that was blackness featuring scenes (indistinct activity, shadowy little people scurrying, or not people), creatures, countenances appearing and disappearing in moments (demonic faces with swirling smiles that morphed into others, with expressions of scorn, with eyes that were glowing points in triangle caves, faces that were expanding tessellated masks). Blackness in which anything might materialize before the mind's eye—a house in disrepair on a windswept prairie; a cackling child with mussy chocolate-colored hair; a rapidly growing tree with spindly leafless branches; a lightning storm lighting sporadically a navy sky; a clown locomoting on a hopper ball; the animated head of a bodiless kitten, a pair of fangs hanging stalactite-like in its open mouth (the head becoming larger, clearer).

In   isolation   so-to-speak   self-imposed,   in

loneliness—aloneness—in a moment of extreme desolation he saw with his mind's eye, in half the duration of a blink, the disconcerting image of a deranged or distraught thirty-ish man, mouth ajar, seeming or involuntarily imagined to be screaming soundlessly and eternally and in the saddest of sad states, a figure he knew was visible only to those who were in such a state of deprivation, by the second-fraction and at the whim of the nightmare man seen.

———◦((◦))◦———

He saw: a defeated man (a man who had trouble admitting it to himself but after many years of being old and alone, self-alienated, decided toward the end this was the case), a Christian, conservative, creationist of six decades; a man who in that time had slowly watched his age become advanced, who'd caught a bullet from a Chinese in Korea while ostensibly safeguarding the world's freedom; who spent his last fifteen years mostly in his living room, in his favorite chair (the seat of which was forevermore a mold of his sizable ass), which was decaying as he was, decomposing inanimate beneath a shrinking semi-animate mammal gone gray and grown saggy: semi-living; mostly dusty, empty, inside; waiting, bodily aches thoroughly distributed his most rousing stimulus; smelling sickly, like stagnation. A man who when moribund remembered more frequently and better than in quite some time being a hale young man, experiencing a detached appreciation for this time in his life, a feeling like viewing a youth on a beach and deriving joy from the fact of the teen/young adult's health and common humanity. Who experienced happiness then because of being at or approaching the culmination of his (Leo Archibald's) terrestrial term, the end of that term's functional suit of flesh and bone, blue blood and elastic meters of intestine, wind bags, life-fluid pump, central computer, various appendages, an assortment of other apparatuses.

Saw: those who sold their plasma—often thin, usually youngish—who afterward were drained sometimes spiritually, maybe mentally, always physically. One with a neon-green bandage around an elbow and sparkless eyes set in brown rings got on the bus and progressed along the aisle a ways and then the bus started moving and he fell into a plastic seat, stringy dark brown hair in his eyes. The mentally handicapped man aboard about twenty-two moved from in front to the back when he saw a young woman a few years older board he found attractive. He wore Coke-bottle glasses and high sweatpants and was somewhat hunched; he carried a kid's backpack of dark green like his sweats and his eyes were set close together on either side of an aquiline nose. He sat near the pretty lady. "My name's Harold, what's your name?" he asked and she answered politely.

"Do you live alone?"

"No, I don't. Do you?"

"Oh, that's cool," he responded a little disappointed. "I live with roommates."

"Me too, I have roommates."

"That's cool. Hey, do you mind if I sit next to you?"

"Oh, no thanks, I'd like to have my space right now."

"Oh, okay."

Another woman in her twenties came on who wasn't hard to look at. He changed seats to sit close to her and the conversation went roughly the same except he didn't ask to sit beside her.

"No, I live with my boyfriend and my two babies, what about you? Do you live alone?"

Another one came on, the same sequence. Three women in a row.

A fat middleaged man of African lineage, overgarbed in late June, developmentally disabled too, came up the front steps heavily. In one hand he carried a filled trash bag and in the other a bulky stereo.

"Do you have a bus pass or bus fare?" inquired the driver.

He tugged at a monthly pass hanging from his neck, the wrong side showing, saying "June, June" but somehow mispronouncing it as he walked on.

"Are you going to show me a bus pass or give me bus fare?"

"June, June." He fell into a seat with a thud, placing the stereo, which there was no room for on his lap or beside him, in the aisle.

"Could you take that stereo out of the aisle so people don't trip over it, please," the driver requested, looking in his passenger-view mirror.

The man(boy) wordlessly obeyed by fitting it, with effort, under his seat.

He wore two pairs of cheap sunglasses. On the rhinestoned, inner pair there was a label on which the name 'Terry Johnson' was printed. The transparent trash bag, occupying the seat to his left, was full of *Personal Power II* audiobooks, all unopened; as he sat he opened the plastic sealing on these, took out the tapes and dropped them in the bag, then dropped the cases either onto the ground or into another bag at his feet. His body or/and clothing gave off an intense, acrid smell discernible at a yard.

An old woman, octogenarian, sat in the middle part of the people carrier, hunched around a purse she gripped with two withered hands. "I spent too long in that antiques shop and it was too musty in there and now I can hardly walk because I can't hardly breathe," she was saying to herself or anyone in earshot. "It used to be that I wasn't allowed to spend too long in one place because they said it wasn't good for me—you spend a lot of time in one spot, bad for health... but"—her voice was sad and trailing off—"...it's not like that anymore."

"I could really use some water if you have some water," she added to no one. Then she rested her head on her handbag on the seat beside her and after laying motionless like that for a while moved to the back.

⸺◈⸺

Sometimes he felt a special awful all over inside and worried he would soon have a full-blown panic attack, which [not counting an alcohol-related freak-out (one day in China he decided he wouldn't and couldn't go to work—because he'd gone to sleep drunk, slept fitfully and too briefly, and woke up drunk and immediately started drinking lukewarm beer from a bottle, one of many stocked up in his apartment, instead of just having a can of beer across from work prior to his first class or during the first sufficiently long break—and went eventually to the nearest hospital instead. And there a staff English speaker was summoned who ended up getting in touch with the liaison between the company he had come to the country through and the school he worked for, a spectacled pregnant woman who showed up unexpectedly after he had spent a long time (or so it felt) in a waiting area bucket seat, many times walking across the street to resupply himself with bottles of beer, needlessly and as part of some kind of self-realized self-detrimental unnecessary farce (like his whole life), from a store that sold the same brand of three-something-percent twenty-four-ounce bottles he'd come in with two of—which he consumed while sitting with relations of the ill, with anxious or sad waiters—and had started the day with. He kept flagrantly getting drunker, at a frenzied pace, before the hospital public—but no one much cared. A doctor in street clothes stopped to call him *xiao jiu gui*. And when at length he had his turn (even though he actually shouldn't have been there) he importuned those attending to him to x-ray his liver for suspected substantial damage. So soon he was lying down shirtless on a cold metal slab, a doctor and blue-uniformed and -becapped nurse on either side of him; the latter rubbed some colder-than-the-slab transparent jelly on the area to be inspected and the doctor used a handheld x-ray while looking at a monitor atop a piece of technology the slab projected from and said it looked fine, and his pregnant acquaintance/colleague the liaison was there and appeared concerned. And they left together, he and the glasses-wearing woman with child, and he was by this point almost blacking out, but out on the street he bounded to the other side to the same store he'd been making trips to for the same product; and she tried to stop him saying he could get hurt, almost ran into the street after him, and he nearly got hit but was half-attentive to the brisk cars. And sometime later he was going in and out of being blacked out as he perilously stumbled up some concrete stairs, enceinte alabaster-skin poor-eyesight woman behind him, in front of him another coworker, who was nervous due to concern for his welfare, whose apartment he was being led to (he recollected having tea there). And back at his place his Australian acquaintance checked in on (having heard about) him and he watched *Leaving Las Vegas* at least once in an alcoholic stupor, feeding off of the feeling of being a drunk), or a similar feeling he'd experienced once after taking a Paxil] he'd had on one occasion (but, funny thing, he could no longer remember exactly when or where he'd been or how it'd come about, though he'd probably been especially stressed. Physical, it was a sensation of intensity that, nausea-like in part, was mingled with (and originated from) strong general anxiety, but far exceeded merely a feeling of great anxiousness).

<hr />

On the frontier of consciousness were new human specimens whose eyes blazed brighter with energy, whose bodies glowed with essence, people more aware and more knowing and often beyond circumstances at peace, like monks who sat motionless as their skin and fat burned—as they died, but only physically.

━━━━━━━━━━‹‹◉››━━━━━━━━━━

He thought of the words of Jefferson Airplane. What had once been his truth had been found slowly, bit by bit, to be fallacies. Many of the lies were quaint; practically all were easy. Within him, the capacity for happiness had died, or anymore was seriously limited. He wanted, felt he needed and had better find someone to love, who loved him (but did he himself?). Wanted what seemed the most important or only important thing he didn't have...maybe wouldn't have, maybe couldn't.

━━━━━━━━━━‹‹◉››━━━━━━━━━━

He detested his job because (among other reasons) it required him to do things that were contrary to who he was, to his ideology/values; because he had to bother, entreat, condition, and lie to strangers. Because he was working willingly for the villains, only one remove from being directly employed by enemies of the environment, all species, by the power- and money-hungry.

He didn't want to get off early though from the job he detested. He didn't because if he did he might not or would not be able to pay rent. He would be utterly fucked; the life he did not like would come to an end—a life that was always

78

imperiled, that he was always a paycheck away from being unable to hold on to. And this imperilment was very worrisome to him, all the more so because it was unlikely he would die as a result of the feared becoming reality; his survival, his life, would become much less comfortable was all, presumably far less tolerable (and it'd long ago reached many others' intolerable). He ought not, perhaps could not quell his worry; possibly if becoming unemployed would have resulted in death, but not if his being jobless merely caused an awful existence to ensue, continued life to become closer to unbearable than his (for him) barely tolerable previous situation, suicide (or otherwise being a victim of homicide) his most likely near-future escape—a way out that was not at all good, not at all right (how terrible it was if, and especially if much too early, the only known escape from a no longer bearable existence was the end of existence, perhaps a self-effected end).

He did not want his present state of affairs, which he was unhappy with, to change—for if it did it would realistically change for the worse, substantially so (he felt). He did not want (much) pain as a man, an animal (pain that would no doubt be emotional and physical), but neither did he want the life he still held on to by a thread and that invoked a degree of emotional pain too. He wanted his life to be a life he wanted or at least didn't dislike. He was as a vermin trapped, a vermin that by its nature wanted its own continuance, was conscious enough to be of the mind its continuance would be solely for the sake of continuing, but did not want to continue on in the trap it had always existed in, wanted life outside of or beyond it. It wanted to go on living but its entire life it had spent in the detested trap (from which there seemed but one escape). It wanted to go on existing but it had only known existence in the trap; so it thought that maybe it could not exist outside of its prison, and perhaps the prison could not exist without him inside it (the prison fed on life perhaps). The vermin wanted life, it did not like the life it seemed to've been relegated to living and always had been living but ultimately wanted life—the vermin wanted to live but did not want to live the only life it had ever known. (It was better, thought the trapped thing, healthier, to want than not to want to live—though it'd matured in many ways into a living antithesis of life. The captive felt little or no loss due to this however; it didn't care and was generally content with itself and its (asocial) bug condition.)

<hr />

(sung—joyously, by an unseen chorus)
Stinky Stew, whiskery, pale green-uniformed homicidal psycho, is coming down for me, for you!

He's always humming erratic classical when he kills—in a murdering campaign!

He's sick, and evil, and evil is sickness, only some sickness evil.

After twenty years he thought he was poison, after thirty-five he meant to be drunk. He's coming down with a blunt tool or a jagged implement for me, for us!

He wants to get kicks from our deaths!

(sotto voce) Stinky Stew is coming...for me, for you...

Then: there was piano music, not harsh but not soft (it wafted in); then the image of a piano became gradually visible, of average size and polished to a gleam, almost too bright, and it came, rather quickly it seemed and in no space, toward Orlan, who seemed to be, felt he was floating, an apparition. *But do I feel like a specter?* he asked himself as he hovered before the near, stationary apparition of a blemishless piano (keys whiter than possible in reality or seemingly lit by bright bulbs not present), not knowing (or really putting much effort into determining) what was going on. Did he still have a head of hair, a tentative white streak in the front? Was he yet clad in a jacket of leather, jeans of denim, and extent physically? Was he a caricature of his own mind, or a larger mind? What had his life been, that is what had it meant, and wait—where the fuck was he? He felt gripped by panic but at the same time incapable of physically experiencing it, the various unique pains, the physical manifestation of the discomfort of the organism (one that had previously been surrounded by genetically similar manifestations of life—all the animate human organisms—pushing one another, damaging one another, crazy, dynamic, diverse, viral, so many diseased. Using so much power and producing so much garbage. So many of them apathetic and malicious and uncomprehending. ...Want and ignorance, those terrible overcoat-shrouded children, governed a multitude—far too many. And many too were those resilient, resourceful; and adaptive (or not). Many were the TV slugs and morning joggers).

(And he thought of how infrequently Henry—whose mind ever since the introduction of him Orlan seemed at times to occupy, Henry whose mind at least was often the focus of the ever-changing dreamscape (Orlan at other times feeling he was thinking as others he saw, imagined, or at least experiencing an unprecedented hyper-empathy that did not disallow disgust and bewilderment, or a grim sense of familiarity, to be felt simultaneously)—had felt remorse rather than or addition to anxiety about external consequences, even if he had rarely wanted to harm anyone physically or otherwise and disliked the idea of harming anyone who had not wronged him.)

———— ((●)) ————

He was unsure if he was able to recognize romantic love, if he was able to ever (or ever again) really experience it. And if he had known it—and never would again—it was early on, briefly in any and all cases, and it only barely (if at all) seemed better for him to have known it on one or more occasions than never; because of the in his experience typical cost, emotionally, of caring about someone to such a degree. Maybe, probably even, there was no such thing as one single true love, and he certainly could not imagine lusting after only one person. He could also hardly imagine being tolerable much less desirable to someone in a longterm monogamous relationship, imagine being in one, that lasted more than a year or so.

There went by on foot, anonymous, as all, a sad, strange little man in an ill mood, who until he became physically ill the next day (just a bout with phlegm and snot, but in a few years he would develop a chronic ailment) didn't realize that he should have that day at least been thankful because he was healthy, and young. This occurred to him and he was grateful, but before he was well again he'd forgotten the thought.

Sometimes he found himself, his life, repellent overall, more than was appropriate to he thought. He had once wondered why (and how) one who basically lost interest in being alive many years earlier would often feel like living on indefinitely, and thought one answer to the former question was sadomasochism, and one (obvious) answer to the latter question was the inborn drive to prolong life. There were things he wanted to do he hadn't, things that were important to him to do, but maybe he was a sadomasochist—someone addicted to experiencing pain, who subconsciously wanted their road to be a painful one—maybe had long been at least a bit of one.

Through action or otherwise a multitude of human lives were being daily deemed valueless by *he*s, *she*s and *it*s (individuals and corporations, governments, other noncorporeal entities staffed by bodily ones but far less palpable, scrutable)—unjustly, mostly for the sake of accumulation (under capitalism people only mattered to the extent they affected profits). Dehumanization was integral to moral/ethical wrongdoing and was often necessary for the success of wars and conquests, just as it was necessary to running a prison; dehumanization was a prerequisite for much of the cruelty that occurred in the world. To effectively manage, kill, plan for them human organisms were best or had to be regarded as like a bunch of stupid, insignificant ants going about practically mindlessly. Defecating, eating, working, fighting, purchasing, vegetating, copulating, sleeping. They—the people, the ants—were the consumers, but they were also potentially the enemy; and in numbers great enough they could be a formidable one indeed, all the more so perhaps because they were largely infantile, imbecilic.

When he was not very old Henry thought overly of women, sex, long-term relationships. He had been in a handful of intimate relationships and for a long time having a girlfriend was one of his main goals, practically the most important thing to him. But in fact the relationships he had had hadn't seemed to particularly better him, his life, in the long run; neither a significant other nor sex was at all crucial (the more sex he had the more he'd want it when he wasn't having it), and in the case of the former he'd come to think maybe he was better off without one, partly because he was so often lonely when not in a relationship, especially for some time after one ended, as always they did—and he desired to become totally, unalterably content with being single.

<hr />

He saw himself or he saw someone else or he saw himself as someone else, or saw through the eyes (the filter) of someone else or himself, Orlan. But Orlan wasn't, was it (he rhetorically asked himself), his only self—only it was the current one, most recent one; or had been (now the fact of his being, being Orlan anyway, continuously, was uncertain—what had happened?). He was oldish or not very (and when not very he thought overly, subconsciously mostly, of aging, of death, of inevitabilities he to an extent had a fondness for, was pleased by the fact of, the indications of which he saw in himself). He was real and not real—that is, always real in the Descartes sense but not always Orlan, not always alive (as a person sometimes he was a spirit(-fragment) in hibernation). He was present or not present, or seemingly present but had entered the mind and also sometimes the body of another person, become someone who had maybe never existed; was one entity and many, but not simultaneously, never did he have concurrent consciousnesses.

It did not matter to the Mesopotamian boy sodomized against his will by two members of the army that had conquered his motherland that a spokesperson for the invading country called the vast majority of this force well-behaved—like those invaders who stormed the house of a sleeping family in the middle of the night, rifles pointed at the occupants' Maglite-lit deathly-frightened faces, to arrest the sixteen-year-old boy who during the day had thrown a rock at a tank; who in the prisons they'd commandeered or built in the desert tortured prisoners (many guilty of no misdeed) in ways bizarre and degrading, rarely very physically damaging but always creative; who accidentally killed large groups of civilians via bomb-equipped planes (but then to the families of the unintentionally murdered, as to the raped, the maimed, said sorry).

⸻

Bad men did what good men dreamt. *Good* and *bad* were words as corrupted as ever or more, often intentionally, and unholy hordes misidentified bad as good and vice versa. Good was what was the best for the environment, humanity's surroundings, including its cosmic environs. The more of a difference the human species was capable of making the more responsibility it had.

Henry thought perhaps he had over lifetimes due to ignorance, due to the ignorance around him, become increasingly degenerated. He wasn't better than most; maybe he was worse, more corruptible, more corrupted.

Sometimes, not frequently, he honestly queried himself, verbally or internally, "What do you think of yourself?" or "What do you think should be done with you?", "How would you respond to yourself?" or "How would you live?" "What actions would you take?" he would ask, never liking the responses, nonverbal, that he started to get. Then he would realize that this sort of self-questioning necessitated or indicated a sort of splitting of a sort schizophrenic, which was of course regarded by him as a little worrying. Who wanted to end up a schizo? To become a real-life Carter Nix?

Sometimes Henry wished people (specific or in general) ill, and for a period always laughed, internally if not alone, when he heard of another gunman, mass murderer—almost always an American in America (often one whose crime was committed in a school or small town)—and, he had to admit to himself, usually (unfortunately) related a bit to the per-petrator, just as he generally related to those who self-ter-minated, like such killers typically did. Grateful were those sick and/or ireful people he assumed that the nightmare of their lives was over early. The sunderer had come to them (they'd summoned it), and finally the astral arose from them for the last time—for it was unattached now to its brother body, rendered an inanimate heap of matter.

―――――‹‹◉››―――――

Later on we'll fly;
For now we're just shadows

―――――‹‹◉››―――――

Life was temporary, fleeting. The ego, more so than the body, was nothing. Always lives were starting, ending, as ev-eryone was constantly in transformation. So went the hu-man cycle—during which the ego like the organism could be born and die—that had been ongoing for eons.

―――――‹‹◉››―――――

Henry daydreamt once that his entire back was com-prised of a physical double of him with wilder hair, an alien attached twin, clothed the same but with a different, quite disparate, demeanor, expression—its face looking like a maniac's, that of a smiley villain ready to lunge.

⸺⫸⫷⸺

He realized consciously, perhaps a bit belatedly, that he was in a rut; he accepted this even, as much as at any given time he could muster acceptance, complacency, resignation. But it was not just a rut—it was the rut that was the life, his life, the life of a peon in poverty; it was his existence (in a substantial way, especially societally), it seemed permanently, for he foresaw no means by which it'd change, except that he would be always a physically and spiritually transmuting organism, a (he hoped) higher animal whose vast inner processes of infinite complexity kept it ever (to the naked eye) invisibly self-altering (physically, after an apex, going into disrepair, deteriorating to an ultimate end). Except that the situation could foreseeably get worse. But presently, oddly, he didn't know how much he desired a change of external circumstances anymore, whatever the implausible more favorable circumstances would be like—even though the place he was at was, he thought, only enviable in that it wasn't street level. Was between rock and hard spot, a despised, self-lowering and -challenging place, a place that caused him to long for positive but unanticipated alteration—the one thing he was particularly grateful for being a small lair that served as a sanctuary much needed.

He tried smiling anymore and the smiles came out forced or painful quite conspicuously; he was beyond the point of put-on ones, now he could no longer successfully pretend them, or pretend normalcy, mental acceptability; he probably oft came across as a little off. He certainly knew firsthand loneliness, neuroses. (Knew the hole. Back down the hole (he frequently went, not by volition), a bit different all the time—into the shifting nightmare, zone of horror, where despite plenty of life one realized sooner or later their isolation (amid diverse sick-making lunacy), that one had oneself only to carry one through, to govern and bear the consequences for one's actions. Back down the hole already occupied.)

Henry felt sometimes he would trade every bit of individuality to be one of the many comparably-aged males of his nation, the majority it seemed, who took their normal life, their attractive (to them and societally) girlfriend, their car, satisfactory job, et cetera for granted (or so he speculated they did in most cases).

He recalled time spent brooding, sociopathic in ill-lit bars, sipping brews, observing in silent sullenness, almost sullenness. Near animals the same type but not. The kind of time that led to his thinking how he had on many occasions been, he suspected, disliked because of his inability (or unwillingness) to join in, be just a functioning component of a group. Because he was not a person who typically fit in, got along; it was difficult, if he tried, for him to do so. He was not adequately socialized, did not have much in common or much fun, didn't or couldn't talk casually, joke with others. At times when he felt this inability intensely he felt pathetic, like a failure, loner, a sociopath or on the road to being one (but he'd spent plenty of time wanting to be that and honing, not so consciously, the set of behaviors (more natural to him than not) he associated with antisocial personality disorder).

He was aware, and ubiquitous were the signs, of being but a drop in an immense bucket; knew the feeling of futility; of being frequently on the verge of weeping, wanting to cry finally for the relief of it but being unable to; of a sadness immense, oppressive—a huge awful sadness the reasons for which were too many to enumerate or know.

Knew badness in people's eyes, people's cold eyes, eyes that didn't care in even a vague human way about other humans except a very few.

Saw everywhere people, crazy, with eyes like this, with gelatinous spirit-portals midnight black—hominids strange, mean in a insane, strange, mean world, taken to lunacy by unnatural, nonbeneficial conditions. Sometimes the sadness, badness, craziness was enough to make someone look forward to the end of their life, make someone feel they just couldn't fucking take it anymore and what the fuck were they going to do...

⸺⋅◉⋅⸺

Fucked up bag of meat and bones. Sad withering creature walks the streets under white streetlights observed by
other creatures less and more sad and withered, more and less
shrunken, hunched, new-formed, well-formed. A retard age
twentysomething, a male four-seven or so, having just exited
a city bus on its arrival at the station, passes and his attention
locks on a fiftysomething transsexual. He says hi and when
the male-to-female transgender briefly makes eye contact he
discerns she isn't going to respond and gives her a conspicuous look-over shoes to crown. He walks jerkily wears thick
glasses and a backpack. Calling to mind the detachment of
the sea the transsexual's eyes are cold, calculating quickly;
she wears a lilac long skirt and matched jacket of a material
like burlap. Everyone's actions and expressions seem overly
interpretable (but is he interpreting them accurately?) and
the night feels infused with malaise.

⸺⋅◉⋅⸺

To get by, to get high, to get drunk, they the face-forgot-
ten drained themselves of precious body fluid, leaving them
feeling each time a little permanently weaker, making each
time their arm-crook scar a little more present. Plasma to go
to the face-ruin of a burn victim, some unfortunate in agony

92

made physical monstrosity, from someone anonymous spiritually and corporeally depleted. Someone who reclined for an hour (after waiting for two) with a thick syringe in them, trying to concentrate on *The Nutty Professor II* (*The Klumps*) while their blood went into a centrifuge then was pumped back into them one component lighter.

———————⟫⟪⟪⟫⟪———————

Days he didn't have money enough to buy weed, or even alcohol, the cheapest store-stocked bottle of wine, he took over-the-counter sleeping pills—he took them at minimum every work night, had developed the habit, dependency, years ago (during a suicidal depression)—earlier than usual: baby-blue diphenhydramine and calcium tablets, usually more than the recommended dosage. Such days of relative lack of funds he always hoped not to have to work, and if he didn't he'd wallow in bed (an ancient mattress on a years-unvacuumed floor) till mid-afternoon half-asleep, depressed (though grateful to be able to do nothing).

He didn't often realize he was somewhat down but signs showed him in retrospect that he frequently was, signs like (perhaps because of not thinking about it) for days not bothering to shower, shave, use toothpaste when brushing; not even giving his teeth a once-over prior to turning in.

———————⟫⟪⟪⟫⟪———————

He felt finally, with self-pity and a sense of its largely self-inflicted truth, that he had become an entity yet young but in many ways living a life different (in a less desirable way) from the better part of those of his age and citizenship: he was internally atypical, an ambulatory creature less alive (more also) and more (self-) governed than the bulk of these others, many of whom he disliked. Just as he disliked the majority of the older and younger adult, and some of the nonadult, compatriots he daily saw and spoke to, the same motherfuckers who mostly voted either Republican or Democrat in every presidential election, for one of two actors, neither of whom would change much (if so not for the betterment of the general populace), both of whom ultimately played for the same side (and it wasn't the side of the people who rather seemed to deserve, due to their sheep similarity, learning disability, most of the bitter fruit of the financially failing (and otherwise) *"democratic" republic*); who mostly (unfortunately) still believed the fairy tale of 3/27 (an event concocted by the world puppeteers, financiers, to serve select governments, industries, corporations)—the tall tale, delivered by big media, indoctrination companies (via their actor employees), that led to sweeping and scary domestic and world changes being instituted and long endless-seeming wars (predicated on a lie, the liars the definition of nefarious) being waged.

———◦(◦)◦———

In a state of the union, deep in one of the United

States—a state with humid summers that made the skin ever damp and mild snowless winters, in which the majority of the adults called themselves Christians and the majority of the men football fans—there lived the foursome of Rick, Charlotte, Shannon and Timmy, residents of a city of some twenty-four thousand, and of a rundown and overly small house beside a lethargic stream always green (over the portion of which was on their property a long row of sickly-looking trees on either bank drooped, the sluggish water always almost entirely in the shade). The parents among this brood (Rick, forty-five, and Charlotte, forty-three) had never had a proper bed in the more than a fifth of a century they had inhabited the dilapidated domicile and in that time, aside from the infrequent necessary repair job (work that papa himself, through trial and error, did on his own), had never improved the place. Patriarch Rick was a mean man by disposition, one which his habitual abuse of alcohol made worse. He was also without conscience and with an IQ only slightly above the moron threshold and Shannon and Timmy, twins, had both been beaten often until such time as they began to resemble adults, when the beatings had subsided then stopped, though it was some time after she no longer received beatings that Rick also ceased raping Shannon, unattractive and twenty, her head a psychological ruin. It might have been true that Charlotte once (at least thought she had) loved her high school sweetheart Rick, always incapable of and unfamiliar with the emotion, but since some time after her long labor, the pushing out of two unfortunates, that had not been the case. By increments, painfully, she had come to regard her previous feelings for him as

95

misguided; she had become bitter, but internally channeled that bitterness, directed it elsewhere, certainly never towards Rick in any way he could discern; had come to hate him, somewhat less passionately though than the kids did. The family (except for Rick—decades from retirement but burnt out—when he was at work) spent practically all their waking hours watching TV; not the kind of programming (despite their seventy-one channels) one stood to learn from other than about current American culture (and anyway their attention spans were comparable to those of mites). And the sorry foursome, the backwater bunch of doom—very much of their time, place, and educational attainment—consumed what their lives were, the equivalent of shit, and also spent a lot of time eating, in front of the viewcube, the progenitors (who spoke little to one another and less to their adult children—who were devoid of aspiration, not counting Timmy's desire to kill Rick, something he commonly fantasized about doing) overweight and their offspring on the road to so being. (And the toxic imitation food they stuffed themselves with in front of the glowy box—from which emanated rubes in love triangles and sun-leathered empty-headed young couples; staged survival shows and vainglorious motorcycle mechanics (they lived a non-life, wishing subconsciously for death)—was full of addictive chemicals and various poisons/ unhealthful additives; was the favored sick-making stuff bought by the socioeconomically unprivileged masses across the nation, the pigs' favorite slop.)

In Iowa an autistic boy about ten lived in a world of his mind. He was a boy whose busy parents loved him but wished he'd been born normal; who would always be a boy, in mind, always live in his mind, a mind that didn't quite work right for most things (but for some things worked better than those of most). He stared hour on hour at the luminous living room corner computer screen, which he touched, kissed, blew at. He was primarily nonverbal; often slapped his cheeks or appeared catatonic, wagged his head like in a trance; was largely uninvolved in human interaction; communication, mostly with his mother and usually instigated by her, was frequently frustrating for one or both parties.

In Washington State Maureen and Dwayne Willis, their lifetime-live-in twenty-five-year-old Ronny, and their youngest, Darla, who had multicolored braces on her teeth—all of whom were obese, Ronny most of all—lived in a three-bedroom house the floors of which were spotted abundantly with pieces and piles of feces that was ancient and petrified, practically coprolitic, to fresh and moist. The living room sofa stationed before the ubiquitous entertainment center centerpiece and hypnotizer smelled like the ass of a dog, one of the three animals (the others cats) the four human ones shared their home with that daily peppered the abode with excrement and urinated wherever they chose, that the paper-mill-employed dad paid to feed, that lived a good life there (besides living in their shit) and were frequently pet. Some nights, both of them drunk, Ronny and a friend play-fought

97

with swords on the back patio using real swords and wearing mail (though not full suits of it), and one day Ronny's
friend sustained a serious abdominal slash but drank it off
as he bled on the dog hair- and dead skin-covered couch
that all four family members were in the habit of lying on,
that the mom watched daytime talk shows and she and her
high schooler daughter watched shows about and starring
hot rich bitches planted on, mostly motionless but for a hand
bringing Cheetos, a Hot Pocket or the like to a mouth (as
internal processes dealt with copious toxins, their gas-tracks
moving methane), that all but the daughter sat on when the
rest of the clan watched WWE (which they believed to be
authentic) while eating messily, drinking, dripping, belching,
expelling mephitic gas. Once the daughter didn't shower for
a week to see how long she could go, but when she was in
the house one couldn't smell her from any distance over the
assaultive aromas of poop and pee. Once the white cat, the
female, gave birth to a litter that died off one by one within
three months of eye infections that spread to their brains, and
which daily sealed their small eyes with goop that Maureen
would clean off, and in the weeks before their deaths drove
them crazy—they would blindly and viciously attack, clob-
ber themselves on walls, mew endlessly, pitifully—and after
each died its tiny corpse was put in a cardboard box that for
weeks the family neglected to dispose of and left open, in the
house (and so it smelled of shit, piss and death). And once
the front doormat, black from filth, was white; and always
there were mounds of dirty dishes and the mounds never
seemed to not be there; and flies were always everywhere
inside, large noisy adults and half-size juveniles, copulating

or feeding on the newer piles of dog and cat shit among the many that were not recent additions; and no matter how close they sat to those they were talking to every one of the Willises was a loud obnoxious talker.

<hr />

The hole that he'd come to was where he would slowly die. The hole that he'd come to to slowly die. He didn't want her to see the hole that he'd come to slowly die in. The hole he'd ended up in to die slowly. The hole where he would slowly die; the hole that would gradually kill him. The hole he was captive in that was the cesspool that was the world, within which he was in a hole that was waiting for him after one-third of sixty-nine years, one-third of a slightly below average lifespan for a modern man (though he mightn't make it that long, doubtless wouldn't make it in good condition). The hole in which he was trapped—a little-known one he'd never have imagined (a hole that was the stink of the Earth, a stench his stink was a part of, a grimy, gray place)—and slowly dying. And he didn't want the beautiful woman (young, younger than he was) to see him in, occupy with him, a pathetic almost nonentity, the hole in which in emotional excruciation he was dying.

She wore green, vernal green the vernal girl, and her apples of cheeks were red on skin tan, her hair auburn and in place, lips voluptuous, eyes big, intelligent, irises beautiful. Legs and ass perfect, hips to make a man hard, and all the rest of her body ideal too, she sat for the time being in the same dungeon and for the first time beside him; and about her as he occupied space so near her (even as he read—tried to read, pretended to read—the newspaper) were most of his thoughts.

———◆———

He'd come to feel it was better to talk to people as little as possible, for a variety of reasons, one of which was to avoid people being assholes. Another was to avoid interacting with people who turned out be assholes in general, and another was to avoid people who reeked of their sickness, sadness.

During beginning-of-shift announcements the supervisor doing them began his thirty-second spiel by saying "welcome to hell." Appropriate he thought, but he also thought "I'm a longtime resident, this is just one of my least favorite parts." Then began the hard job of an ordinary day, which turned out to be an exercise in serenity (not for the first time), due to the fact some douchebag was sitting beside him.

That night he saw the woman he'd been dating; the night before his roommate, unasked, gave him two of the (nonrefillable) twenty Vicodins he'd received because of his severely sprained ankle. He had watched the film *Jindabyne* quite high from the one and a half he consumed after putting a microwave burrito and some slices of roast beef in his stomach. He drank most of a pot of coffee then started drinking orange juice, vitamin D-fortified, smoking a cigarette at least every twenty minutes. He laid down for bed at about three, finally falling asleep for good sometime after four. He dreamt of spiders biting the crooks of his arms, his fingers being pieced by hot sewing needles, performing poorly at his shitty job, a conversation with someone who hadn't been in his life in twelve years in which he was defending himself but had not been attacked. In the late morning when he woke his roommate was watching YouTube clips of road rage real and make-believe. At work the woman sitting behind him and a few stations to his right was wearing a shirt that displayed thankfully much of her sizable, kissable breasts. He had had two beers before he went in and felt slightly hungover from the pills of the previous day.

⚒

Sitting on the front patio of a bar, one he was now again frequenting, his body half in the August sun, the back of his neck exposed to it, he was looking at people passing—some coming from behind, some from in front of him. (A middle-aged man with a backpack leaned on the low stone wall in front of the younger observer that marked off the premises, also presumably people-watching, wearing sunglasses.) He could overcome his natural inclination to look at people in his view—which, because of a peculiarity, among many, was what he typically did—but mostly, this time, didn't choose to; however, when eye contact every so often occurred he broke it off, such as with a woman around his age walking a dog who (he thought) locked eyes with him from some distance and a girl of sixteen or seventeen with a perfect body who was walking with her less desirable similarly-aged sister

101

or friend and two dull adults around a quarter-century their elders. There was nothing dull about the girl's tight-clothed body but for at least one reason, a better one than why he had not kept looking at the woman, he didn't look twice at her, only the first look informing him how wonderful her body was. Segue to a daydream or not quite that of two girls same age equally flawless bodies in a locker room shower, both nude, facing each other, not insubstantial pairs of breasts pointed perky toward each other, asses ideally curved, rivulets cascading down them, over contours streams flowing— petite physically superlative girls, one's shoulder-length hair dark brown, the other's blonde. They began to French kiss and soon were kissing like they were trying to consume one another's tongues, groaning and growing wet. The blonde broke off, licked the other's lips, sucked awhile on the brunette's lower lip, then started thoroughly kissing her counterpart's body—chin, space between her collarbones, space in the middle of high-set breasts, her erect nipples, down her chest, kissing her flat abdomen all over, kissing her navel (an outtie), kissing down to her inguinal depressions, a small patch of pubic hair, to a small sheath like a recently bloomed flower exquisite and aromatic; a beautiful pink place into which the hungry girl water running down her celestial form pressed her tongue as much as she could as the other fully blushed and her vagina relaxed around the muscle, soon tightening around it, and (lips around lips, moaning, making girly noises, breathing heavily, her head back, a hand on the straight blonde shoulder-length hair at the tops of her lightly freckled slender thighs) she approached her first orgasm, while the one pleasuring her inhaled her inner fragrance, tasted her delicious feminine taste, drunk with lust, intoxicated by the taste of the pulchritudinous young woman who was moments from climax. Segue to: the bus after bar number two. Amazingly there was a completely sexually arousing young woman sitting in front of him with a head of straight flaxen hair that fell on a red-white checkered shirt who, though he didn't see her face, he could tell he'd want to kiss every inch of—as he could tell that intercourse with her even briefly would probably cause him to shoot a huge wad inside her all too quickly, as he hungrily, happily, feverishly, kissed the aesthetic animal's face, lips, neck, his fully engorged cock in her vise-grip little pink perfect pussy between slim shaven pink legs that presently showed from white short shorts and which she was bracing against the seat in front of her, giving him a tantalizing view of these; and in addition to her he could also not look left without imagining coitus with a sexually flawless entity, because there sat a girl also seventeen eighteen, also blonde, *maybe* nineteen, wearing a tight plain gray tee over her firm b-cups. And he knew the magnitude of the appeal of their magnificent young bodies, knew his carnality could hardly be more piqued than by these fellow animals and that this was normal for a sexually potent youngish animal; but he buried his consciousness to the extent he could in Burroughs—in boys having sex with boys, men having intercourse with boys, men fucking men, and when he looked up again from the book the girl in front of him was gone and seconds later it was his stop (he went to solitude of self in his precious unadorned cave). At home, home with a battle-scar star, he had the radios in his living room and bedroom tuned to different AM stations. For the

103

nth time he burned himself between the fingers, index and middle, when his cigarette, in this case a rollie roach, slipped while between them. The butt burned away toxic in the glass ashtray, carbon monoxide going into his dying lungs.

PART THREE

I

HENRY AS A young child regularly experienced sleep paralysis. Suddenly his eyes were open and he was screaming voicelessly in odd hours of the night and held in tormented captivity within a rigid body, back tight, muscles contorted (looking like an aerial shot of hills but rippled flesh)—his inability to vocalize psychological, fear-induced; feeling a foreign presence.

━━━━━◦((◉))◦━━━━━

Hookers giggled outside a low-end club, their butts pleather (or leather) -covered, wearing pleather or leather high-heel boots that came up to the tops of their calves or higher, looking across the bleeding-with-energy street to the foreigners, Americans, who in this not-so-diverse segment of the seven-million-strong city were something of an oddity, meant money.

Everywhere were dogs, many dying, many with rabies, most shaggy or scabbed, with hairless patches or open sores, deteriorating visibly and with rapidity.

A smell like everything was in the air, only shit easily distinguishable. Everywhere were unflowing open sewage canals (klongs), a putrid aroma emanating from them—even beside open-air restaurants, the patrons of which dined at white plastic tables on the broken sidewalk, seated on chairs of white plastic.

One might pass and probably miss a small frog on the edge of a sewer drain. Roaches scurrying across the wet walkway, scavenging among trash.

Even in the dry season dirty water streamed across the street, trickled from overhead, and one was always watching out for it draining from somewhere.

He picked up girls, but with broken, simplified English, not Thai; he made them resort to what little English they knew if they wanted him for sex or an ulterior motive.

He woke up in Susawatchi Hotel, but he didn't know that, only knew he was in a bedroom. Who were these girls, the overweight one with lots of eye makeup who was laying beside him, the prettier, older one who was sleeping on the other bed; *where am I, and how did I get here?*—but quickly the answers, if not the whole story (some pieces lost to alcohol), came back to him.

It was late morning, nearly noon, when they woke—he quite hungover, a Michelle Yeoh movie on TV. This they watched awhile; then one sister, the pretty one, flipped around, stuck with BBC.

"I like BBC," exclaimed the other.

After a while her sister surfed again. On another network President Bush the recentest and wifey, all glamorized, like you could see the excess makeup on their faces, proceeded slowly down a red-carpeted staircase while being watched, photographed, and filmed by a multitude. The fat one, sitting up in bed beside him, gave the screen a middle finger.

He woke up in a smothering, sweltering room in Bangkok. He kept reminding himself Thailand, Bangkok, Thailand; asking himself: where in the hell is Thailand? How the hell did you get yourself here? Who the fuck are you?

He recalled the night world of Khao Sarn Road, a place like the Old West choked with hedonists. Drenched in colored lights, filled with bars, restaurants and tourists, with the progression of night tourists more drunk and ill-behaved. Men handing out glossy cards advertising ping-pong shows. Aggressive tuk-tuk drivers parting crowds; a bevy of prostitutes of assorted quality, not all of them (natural) women.

Tiny lizards came frequently, stealthily, into his apartment (here called a *mansion*), a single room not counting the bathroom (wetroom)—moving with subtlety, gracefully, wagging their tiny tails, moving their fragile necks right, left to look, little apprehensive about humans.

What he'd come to deduce was a dog barked endlessly at close and seemingly precise intervals, in spurts, each identical utterance sounding uncannily like "fuck face." The dog did its vocalizing only at night however, the previous night till just past dawn.

He perceived the Thai as a more natural and resourceful people than those mostly of Western European extraction he had previously spent his entire life among and was one of, and he guessed this might broadly be true of Asian peoples, in comparison with those of America, the West. He felt that they were, generally speaking, an example of humankind at its somewhat barer, that theirs was a society less removed from nature, that they were a people more in touch with their own (human) nature.

Here, without consciously choosing to and almost imperceptibly, he became a part of a little disparate community of Westerners, colleagues his age—a group he felt was not cut out for him (if any then could have been or could have been felt to be) that he nonetheless accepted, because they were traveling companions; but no doubt their companionship or friendship was a bigger reason, his ability to talk to them unproblematically.

One morning on awaking he discovered stinking puddles of recent, but already solidified, diarrhea across the wetroom floor, under the showerhead, though little or no trace of the vomit he remembered his body violently and unexpectedly ejected simultaneously (there were only traces of older vomit), as he tore off his sweaty boxers so as not to continue shitting and staining them, in the middle of night, when bad things happen—in Bangkok and elsewhere—when dreams happen (illogical, unpleasant, adventurous, enjoyable): bizarre, frightening, full of longing, insecurities, worries sometimes less than loosely veiled.

What he hardly remembered was that his heavings were dry save much stomach acid, his throat, huge tonsils guarding the entrance, feeling chemical burned, turned inside out, in the early morning (seven-thirty), fifteen minutes to prepare for work, feigning normalcy, even formality; or his introductory puke—off the side of the bed, that old, learned, so recently recalled, still sickening spot—actually two initial regurgitations, resulting in two heaps of vomit; one comprised of his typical lunch, and the other an excessive snack, *gui* and noodles, all green with surprisingly undigested spinach and orange intact carrot gratings.

Unfortunately being an alcoholic was about vomit—expelling it, living in it, taking dark notice of what you coexist with and, as with being a junkie potentially, about diarrhea. He'd imbibed, unrelentingly, until he'd brought himself to quite the level of drunkenness the previous night; lost his room key; nearly passed out on the concrete outside the building in front of one of his few Thai acquaintances, an employee at the apartments (lowering himself physically and in the young man's eyes); and pointlessly but cunningly (detestably) yet again threw an empty beer bottle (nth of the outing) from the tuk-tuk speeding back from tourist-occupied temptation hotbed Khao Sarn: the perfect lucid lost weekend for the perfect subject—"it sucks you in" as someone said to him ("the road" did, Khao Sarn).

Yes; after the first, maybe second trip to a bar called The Hole in the Wall, but especially by a bar called Gulliver's (a place that was only open at night, with a primeval feel at night: the crowd, the dark, the beams above sporadically, unnaturally coloring the crush, blaring music often techno, the dancing fine prime women and lascivious young men, everyone the whole time drinking). It was there or elsewhere on "the road" or near that he met the majority of the women he slept with, working ones and otherwise.

⊷⊶((◉))⊷⊶

TV was a bunch of (Thai or Chinese) soap operas, which—save sports and news—were almost the only programming it seemed. In China it was a bunch of period dramas; Chinese movies (a lot of them cheesy, a lot of them kung fu films); soap operas, Chinese and Spanish and dubbed; table tennis and badminton tournaments; CCTV-9, all news (*xinwen*), the only channel in English. Also breast enhancement cream and exercise machine commercials, the former being used by Henry as a masturbatory aid more than once, while he experienced feeling pathetic as a result.

But most of the time onanism wasn't necessary. In Bangkok there was Suda, who he remembered regaining consciousness in the midst of fucking, their bodies feeling almost permanently attached—a feeling of ecstasy, of perfection; a feeling viscous; of unity, that ended, was replaced by a feeling awful, when he reluctantly eased out upon orgasm, he almost always feeling empty immediately thereafter.

And Narin. Whose hot mouth he remembered on his cock, around the whole cock—but she would never blow him for long and she never wanted him to watch. She had a slim body and firm flawless Bs, alcohol and shellfish on her breath when she arrived nights.

"I love fucking you," he remembered Narin, on top, saying—his very erect cock going in and out of her as she bounced up and down on it, both of them totally nude, the nipples hard on her handful breasts—in the late morning or early afternoon, a while after waking after a very late night spent screwing like bonobos; and he recollected for some reason his face in response read vacuity, displayed a lack of expression (perhaps because as a way for him to deal with his

111

joy he disassociated from it a bit for a moment). In a cheap small hostel room cramped by a bureau and TV, *yaba* (literally "crazy drug") still in their systems that had been provided by Narin's friend, a big-busted world-wise Thai woman with a prominent mole on her forehead (whom he'd wanted to fuck when he'd met her and when he approached her he met Narin, who'd been with her. They made out on a busy side street of Khao Sarn but didn't fuck that first night, just fell asleep together from all the beer (in fact he didn't remember kissing on the curb there, he was blacked out), but wanted to in the morning and he pulled her pants off violently, breaking her anklet (he later replaced it); and that afternoon after he'd gotten her highly turned on in her cousin's bed above his hairstyling shop they did, their intercourse almost spiritual. She was flushed and they were half-naked half-covered by bedsheet afterwards and he was breathing hard and smiling, amazed, still on top on her, and she said "You just come in me," and he shook his head, kind of saying "Yeah," and she said, "You don't have disease?" almost a statement, to assure herself, and he said "No" assertively, and he'd rolled off and she left for the shower and when she came back her hair was wet, it fell to her shoulders, her slight body in a white cotton towel held with one hand at breastbone, she was still afterglow, and they kissed and caressed lying on their sides on the mattress on the floor, and the room through the curtains above was flooded yet with soft yellow sunlight at midday, as it had been during their ideal, spontaneous consummation)—on the one-person bed, in one of the thin-walled rooms meant for fuckers, floaters, squatters, which in the morning maybe later they awoke atop: his hard-on against

112

her little ass, his lips against her hair; and he'd started fucking her like that with pelvic thrusts like the fluid movements of an odd organic machine ("I like it like that," she said; "So do I," he agreed after he'd come). They fell asleep coming and they'd woke coming—and he smelled of her and she of femininity, intoxicatingly. They came together, and she came and came, and she wanted to a fifth time but said she was sore, but before they stopped they came again (she convulsed, in a paroxysm of pleasure almost otherworldly, vagina tightening around the base of his cock). At some point he was going slowly in and out of her small wet pussy and she said "I wish we could stay like this forever" and internally he'd agreed.

⸺⊙⸺

He remembered the hairy-cunt-having cunt he unluckily picked up one night (he temporarily a sex addict) who wore sunglasses in bed, in the dark, as Henry ate out her pussy (unable to do anything else for failure to get it up), encompassed by an overgrown black forest, and stole a one thousand-baht bill from him—in the morning before he woke, then snuck out—the only money he had for the next week. He told his buddy Derek about it, hoping for his help. "You're my wingman," he had told Henry in explanation for covering him for a previously planned sex- (and beer-) fueled Sukhemvit weekend, that weekend, based in Bier Garten and during which they stayed in the classy Nana Hotel.

He fucked three girls that weekend: one slim, ideally slutty, her eyelashes coated with mascara. He met her in Bier

113

Garten where at a low back table he asked her if she liked sucking cock and she said yes, and they sixty-nined each other most of the time and after dressing she did a little sexy dance and legs apart asked him if he wanted to go down on her again, and he got down on his knees beneath her, pulled her underwear aside with his hand and lapped at her wet pussy, head under her short skirt. One who was eighteen, with braids with plastic beads of many colors intertwined in them, huge tits, who under covers without a condom he blew an enormous load into (each hand gripping a monster mammary) after a short time and as soundlessly possible since Derek was in the bed across the room; in the morning Derek asked her "How much?" a little roughly or too businesslike and she seemed slightly scared or somewhat worried and prompted again she finally softly answered five hundred. (Another night soon after in the same area the prostitute, who was twenty years older and had a lazy eye, who'd been with her when he'd picked her up noticed him. "I know you. You take my friend," she'd said in a manner that had an undercurrent accusatory and ominous.) And: a lovely woman about thirty probably, a mole on one of her hands below the thumb, whose fingers he was kissing by the end of their meeting. And soon they were in his room at the Nana and deep kissing with a desire like hunger, and with the same voracity sixty-nining and fucking, then making out more and lying next to each other for minutes that extended beyond the hour he'd paid for, until she finally went, though he did not want her to go, he did not want to stop kissing her, and she'd seemed to really like him too, and he hoped she had some idea how he felt about her, and he thought she did, and she seemed a little sad as she went, and he felt very sad, and afterwards he felt happy and sad (and subconsciously he accepted, appreciated, the brevity of their time together, their flash intersection, and knew it was all it could have been).

———⪼((◉))⪻———

Ko Chang (Elephant Island): Henry and buddies Max and Eric met an Australian guy in his fifties with a permanent residence on the island—who spent half the year making big bucks with an oil company in Oman, where, as he said, "there's nothing but sand and oil"—and his devoted girlfriend, Elle, who was a few years older than Henry.

"Who was the greatest actor of all time?" he queried his juniors, also American-born, as they sat eating sandwiches and drinking beer at a table near the brine. "Rock Hudson. It was Rock Hudson," he answered himself. "'Cause he was gay!" (laughter...the ocean's godlike voice audible in the night).

The five of them shared a joint as they walked leisurely in the sand—the sea, which as always was lapping the earth, only visible as infinite blackness, like space but starless— conversing amiably. "I haven't done this in a *long* time," said the older man, his night-drenched orange skin leathery, as he took the marijuana cigarette.

Later he asked them to figure out a PS2 game for him because, he explained, he just got it, and the system, but he and Elle had been stuck—and they were young so they'd know. Inside his bungalow were copious enormous photographs of an airbrushed Elle wearing makeup, lingerie, and with various hairspray-petrified coiffures, absurd glamor shots on all walls sexy enough—due to the poses, due to how revealing they were—to raise a dick; she had a great body. Max and Eric tried out the game, a racing one, on a TV with an absurdly large screen; Henry unfortunately, pathetically, experienced a feeling of envy with regard to the well-off Australian; and after a fairly short time the man from down under with the straw-colored hair and deeply lined skin, who (along with his girlfriend) might have been an empty vessel, seemed to grow uncomfortable, undergo a change of mood, and thanked Henry's compadres for telling him how to play the video game and essentially kicked the trio out.

⸻ ((◉)) ⸻

His first time to Ko Pha Ngan Henry met a girl on the beach not long after arriving—separating himself from the others (Max and an ache-scarred American he regarded as at best a quasi-bitch) shortly after getting out of the boat—as she accumulated shells along the shore, putting them in a blue pail. He began to help her. They walked along, talking, their dialogue easy. She was a fairly quiet woman, but friendly; attractive but not remarkably so. She wore mascara and had a slim, sexy body; she struck him as especially natural, unpretentious. "I don't care about that," he'd said in regard to sex (probably true at that moment) when the topic came up. "I can tell," she'd said.

He tagged along as she briefly shopped the beach-side

116

trinket stands. Later that afternoon he had intercourse with her in his nearby rented bungalow when she came out of the shower wearing a white towel, her black hair damp and stringy: she rubbed his nipples with much concentration, rendering them sensitive, them and him hard—until he couldn't take it anymore (he hadn't masturbated in over a week; before meeting her was already quite horny), put her on her back on the bed, and fucked her without a condom, the wind (which was blowing the thin fabric in front of the window toward them) lightly felt; a briny-sandy smell from the sea (the Gulf of Thailand, visible from the window, in which later during that trip he was scraped up—the same day he was burnt to the point he was the color of a lobster) coming through the curtain; the dusk, the ocean's propinquity esthetically enhancing their coitus in the dim oceanside cabin ("I don't want a baby," she'd said shortly before he came. "I'll pull out," he'd responded). And he finished on her brown stomach at the last moment and she laughed and touched it as he remained half-propped over her, then he went into the bathroom—actually a wetroom—for some toilet paper and she took it saying thank you and wiped it off.

The next morning Max said "Someone said she had something." She had said she'd just gotten out of the hospital was Henry's first thought.

"I hope you get it," the American woman he came with said. He mulled this over for hours, the cruelty of it (and why?), and hated her for it, hated her ugly rotten-toothed face.

"You used a jimmy, right?" asked Max.

"Yes," Henry lied, feeling unconvincing (not being a

much-experienced liar).

(He was intermittently concerned about this revelation—hearsay—but this faded quickly (as he was, after all, to a degree greater than some or many, insane).)

———— ((●)) ————

Ko Samui: He spent hours making out in the rain with a woman he picked up in a neon-lit bar filled with easy women, with whom he migrated eventually to the beach, who he groped and kissed knee-deep in the ocean. Max ended up with a crazy quasi-prossy, reasonably hot but a bit trashy-looking, whom they'd met (who'd marked them) right after they'd arrived, who in the king-size bed the four shared fought with Henry and the girl whose lips he'd been sucking, who at length he'd been french kissing, in the night-surf and portly-drop precipitation and threw his shoes into the sea in the morning before he awoke, leaving him to go back to Bangkok in flip-flops he begged from the staff of the bungalows, one of which Max and he were staying in.

The previous night there he'd acquired an extremely sexy whore who he sixty-nined in the bathroom and unintentionally underpaid five hundred baht (having told her earlier he couldn't afford her price, though she came anyway); and she seemed unhappy and sad when she left in the morning, most of the hour prior having been spent kissing and sucking on her amazing breasts (after putting on an orange-colored condom and then being unable to get it up).

He remembered thinking he was unable to focus on the whole picture, only on the smallest details, because the world at any given moment in any given place was too much (such as the streets of Bangkok, where it didn't help that all living things were allowed life/to coexist, one reason the tableaux of that place tended toward fullness).

He remembered punching one of the yellow and green taxis stalled in the heavy night traffic off Khao Sarn, drunk, after the Gulliver's doormen (almost never the case) wouldn't let him in without ID, which he was rarely asked for so rarely brought—doing so with all his (unjustified) rage and strength and seeing the huge dent it left in the side before he continued briskly along through the throng progressing beside the vehicle clog. Eric, whom he'd gone with, later informed him he witnessed the event and that not only did he punch the cab right in front of a cop but the driver at once exited the vehicle scanning the crowd for him with eyes baffled and crazed. "He looked like he wanted to kill you, man."

He remembered in one titty bar he went to with Max and Derek there was a cage filled with thirty or so topless and sexy young women eighteen to about twenty-five, barefoot and wearing numbered super-miniskirts (pick a number and the girl came over), ambling across the space in a jumble of others or moving casually to music, some looking despondent. He sat close, in the second tier of seats, and as he drank beer from a bottle he kept watching a blonde-highlighted short-haired beautiful creature with perky perfect breasts, making eyes at her (he had chosen her, subconsciously then consciously, animally). One behind the other the ladies walked around the circle of the cage a few times, a final exposition, then exited; and she came and sat on his lap and he kissed her lips and neck (though she wasn't exactly warm to it), and she had sweet, sad eyes (lips soft, spare body almost quivering), and he sensed how tragically used she was and had been, comprehended she had been transformed externally into (perhaps even innerly, through such conditioning as he was contributing to) an object—"She likes you," Max had said laughing after up there she had become aware that Henry was looking only at her and then looked only at Henry—and he gave her a meager twenty baht before they left, the others telling Henry to hurry up as they headed out; twenty baht to use her body briefly, for a few minutes' mostly illusory intimacy (and he was reminded of how he must've long ago heard the phrase *sex object* and gotten off on it; before masturbation—when he was very young, eight or so—when Henry used to devise extended falling-asleep fantasies featuring himself and two generically good-looking women in their early thirties of the sort he found attractive, one blonde, one brunette, who went by names he had for them as well as "sex object," not even understanding what it meant (but knowing the context). And he would pseudo-dream of Melanie Griffith in *Working Girl* and Kirstie Alley in *Sibling Rivalry*, and Madonna in *Dick Tracy* (a movie for a time as a boy he was obsessed with), who after his initial viewing of that film he more than once at bedtime prayed to God above in all earnestness and with much intensity for from the dark of his room, the black, starry night out the window adjacent to his bed, promising to do anything to have her—what that meant too, to what exact purpose he didn't know—to have her just once; even that young he was that sexually minded).

———⚙———

Back in Oregon following a year in New York he had rested (or tried to), living half the time, in two-week intervals, in Portland and spending the rest of the time in his hometown. He smoked pot and drank a lot (practically constantly), tried mushrooms, did coke again, and was generally bored, dispirited, and allergic to thought. After five months of lazy hedonistic yo-yo life he found himself to his surprise in Thailand, where he lived, also dissipatedly, from May to March.

———⚙———

You lay in the total blackness of the room you just moved into in Staten Island, on a bed in a space empty except for a box spring and a bare, dingy mattress (and overlarge old chest of drawers lined with also-ancient newspaper covered with rodent dung pellets)—no light, no sheets, no other furniture.

You wake up hungover in a one-room apartment in the humidity and heat, sweltering—sweating, in the dark, in every way alone—asking *What am I doing here?*

Being an alcoholic meant getting up in the middle of the night and, while still asleep, peeing on the wall behind your bed; collapsing onto your bed and at the moment your sorry body hits the bed puking over the side of it, then not cleaning it for months; it meant vomit, lots of vomit: vomit your lady friend and her visiting sister find when they come home before you concealed under the covers on the bed, vomit full of complimentary spaghetti you'd received on *Sopranos* Monday at the Greenwich Village bar the three of you had gone to earlier, that mixed with beers you had three of real quick, the last two of which you chugged secretly in your "room" (part of the living room partitioned off for privacy from the rest of that part of the apartment by a large wool blanket), the third of which you forced yourself to finish on top of cocktails (you retching wretch) and many beers you'd had previously; vomit on your black work slacks when you wake on a Friday morning a few minutes before you must leave to get to work on time, your face stuck to the bathroom floor with it, half your semiconscious body in the room half out (the previous night having consumed a forty of something, Old E—then Glenfiddich (which you'd never had before but liked) on ice soon thereafter), and realize you can't call in and must show up.

He remembered...being in a bare room with the lady friend he would soon be living in Brooklyn with. They were sitting on the plastic-covered mattress in the East Village dorm he had had for only a few weeks and would have for only a little while longer. It was a short time after she'd arrived from Oregon and they'd just been sitting there kissing; and she had said, "We can't just sit around here and make out all the time."

———— ((○)) ————

Long before he was an agoraphobe he became a xenophobe. He realized after the fact that was what he had become during months (in the aftermath of a lengthy drug binge) spent in subterranean homelessness, in which period he came to feel apprehension toward people, strangers, to loathe them; to be socially awkward, feel unnatural. But it made sense to him under the circumstances: he was a dissociative-addled transplant, an outsider among his collegiate community—a stranger who was garbed in dirty clothes and showered infrequently, who was barely surviving and yet happy to be there, while most every other student at his institution was well-off comparatively, hip, better adjusted, and probably took their good fortune somewhat for granted.

———— ((○)) ————

He recalled headaches that produced rather than pain an

unpleasant numbing sensation that radiated from the center of his brain to the forehead, making him feel lethargic and dumb.

Neurons telling nerves throughout his body to fire while he was in bed trying to sleep, causing involuntary twitches that roused him from the threshold of slumber.

In the morning signs of overindulgence instead of memory. A shattered wine bottle on the pseudo-balcony. A shallow scratch across the bottom of his left palm he noticed on the toilet.

———⟫(●)⟪———

Henry found he was living in an intangible prison, from which he couldn't escape (or could he?—if he could stop dreaming, so thinking of it), discovered that a mind loose is hell.

He needed to escape from the mind, his mind, to use it only constructively.

At the moment Orlan occupied his own bad dream. The situation seemed, he thought, to be emanating from his mind, but it was perhaps an illusion, fantasy, that originated outside of—as if being beamed unremitting into—it. In either case it was an unceasing nightmare, or more accurately voidmare, though it too (of course), the void, may have been dreamstuff, the creation of a dream that felt like it'd been ongoing for an extended time (as dreams tended to), weeks, months; which was in actuality only occurring during a few moments' eye-flicker.

He thought of Keen, then about the name. One meaning of *keen* was a loud lament for the dead. Maybe he was dead; maybe his spirit was trying to communicate that to itself, or others were. He couldn't remember having ever learned this definition. He thought, Who would lament my death? Not me.

II

Endtroducing Henry Schlesinger/Some of the Hole

HE TOLD HIMSELF he had to change—he'd grown into a despicable person of frequent alarming behavior—even though it was perhaps too late for him. He told himself he was incredibly self-destructive, worthless, criminal. He was the empty eyes of just a shell. That he wanted to be granted peace (but would he allow it?).

He was watching an NBA highlight show and eating peanut M&Ms. He didn't remember all of the previous night but he was roughed up by five guys about his age, Africans, one of them an acquaintance (a happening he instigated due to drunkenness and boredom), and threw a glass against a wall in the bar and fell chin first on the street adjacent, where after some period of time he was awakened ("What are you doing?" "Oh...I'm just sleeping." "You shouldn't sleep here, man. It's dangerous"). He also remembered publicly sobbing and making arrangements with a Muslim friend who worked at a restaurant he frequented, its specialty goat, to get a prostitute the next night, in about three hours. He looked pretty good, normal, more than passable. It felt almost like he had a cracked rib because it hurt when he coughed but he was fairly certain it wasn't. The body assigned him held up well. He couldn't even remember the last time he was sick. The weekend before had definitely been a lost one, spent at bars or fucking. He recollected having told a Chinese guy, middleaged, to fuck his mother because he was annoying him and wouldn't understand, but it seemed as if the guy had ascertained that he had been insulted. Later, almost blacked out, he stole fire extinguishers from various floors of his apartment building, hid one, and threw the rest out windows—once, he thought, hitting a parked minivan. Fuck minivans anyway, he said to himself. That was Monday.

His whitening toothpaste seemed to be working. His behavior was insane, likely uncorrectable, and he'd done many bad things. Sometimes people noticed that something was off. He wouldn't've done bad things if he weren't a drunk; things would have been less interesting though. The next day he was seeing the girl he'd been dating, whom he fed a lot (as one might a pet) and presented with small gifts. They watched soap operas; in an alternate universe they whiled away hours completely alone with each other engaged in sexual activity (rather than zoning out on TV, communicating with difficulty). They walked wintry West Lake arm-in-arm and she told him it was her favorite season, and that her favorite color was blue. He'd gotten good at having simple conversations in Chinese and was relatively well-off. No work that week and he was happy about it. He was moving to a southwesterly province. He required serious psychiatric help. There was no way he could recall all visions and twisted truth, and no escape. (Internally he said) by riding the edge he felt not dead—because it was usually painful, was a challenge that preoccupied him. His history of criminal activity was lifelong...

He remembered dear ol' dad, dear dad fuckhead's

activated charcoal vomit (vomit had played a significant role in Henry's life) spewn across the lawn, black on green with an esophageal sheen (he was back from the hospital after ODing); his stumbling in the yard trying to walk from his wife's car to the front door, crawling through dog doo, the shit on the lawn mostly dry (the grass tended to be too), falling inside. A bounty of beer cans found hidden in the living room wall that meant years of clandestine drinking. While quite young discovering him viewing a porno that featured many very pregnant and lactating nude women by a pool shooting streams of milk at one another boisterously and watching it awhile secretly, perilously, from the top of the stairs (able to see the TV but not his father)... A story about a drunken soldier passing out in the morning in front of the third-world brothel he'd just contracted gonorrhea in; a lovely mountain view; a twelve-year-old Mexican girl getting the shit fucked out of her by a donkey (her day job), pain on her face, palms on her knees bracing herself; cold fingers on hard nipples on Easter Day in tall, scratching bushes (among chaparral chill teats); freedom on the road, going nowhere; a diminutive ex-con from Elko, Nevada, the shithole of the universe, who left a snotty Kleenex on Henry's Greyhound seat because he wouldn't move his seat up the whole time—because he was already cramped himself—even though the man kicked it and cursed like a small child the whole time; pathetic preadolescence; adolescence (terrible haircuts and clothes, riding alone at the fair, being bullied); spitting out pieces of teeth; perfumed neck and hair, his nose buried in hair aromatic, hair against his neck and toes touching in hours-long coitus (until unpleasant disconnection—with mutual disappointed moans, after a time cherished and too brief—a little more difficult for the stickiness), the unyielding suction of bodies together in blackness, tongues convening as he and his lover semiconsciously humped, her hips in rhythm with his slow pumping—fucking blacked out, kissing her face everywhere, sucking on earlobes, tracing silver-dollar-wide areolas in saliva, wanting to feel and taste as much of her body as possible and being wanted to; spilling the offering basket in the sanctuary of the church he grew up going to because he was looking at a pretty girl; thinking about all the people he had made eye contact with once in life and never would again, about his illusion of self-concern, welfare, morality; being asked by people if he wanted to die and sometimes responding affirmatively; an old addict named Art who lived in a van down by the river, a young addict named Larry who was acne-scarred and blind, a blind gray-haired obese and diabetic pot dealer named Kendra whose hurried hoary husband didn't even know she sold weed though she kept it in the freezer; smoking salvia 10× extract and the small bedroom of a friend becoming segmented into fourteen equal pieces, each of which he robotically directed his attention to, singing "it's just the greatest feeling that I've ever had" over a stereo-blared CD, the lyrics of the song playing having nothing to do with the phrase he scream-sung, in addition to the words "it's just so perfect"; stealing his mother's bowl of bran cereal very early in the morning while noctambulating as a toddler, getting in bed, pouring it all over himself and wallowing in the soggy flakes. In eighth grade having a girl-friend named Amber who was ugly and a girlfriend named Crystal who was Hispanic and fine, neither of whom he ever

129

kissed (and both of whom he hardly spoke to); trying to set a teacher's office on fire by igniting a pile of papers on their desk; writing detailed and incredibly raunchy descriptions of homosexual sex acts between members of the staff in most of one set of biology books and getting found out and then his science teacher who featured in them all along with the vice principal calmly asking Henry to step out of class and then backing him into the lockers and spitting red-faced into his face that he had never been so disgusted in all his life; a fight in which he kneed his adversary repeatedly in the balls and it seemed to have no effect and his jeans got muddy.

⸺⸺≈«◉»≈⸺⸺

One morning on the way to work at eight-thirty in the visible pollution, in the gray morning, there was a lot more foot traffic and congestion than usual. And then he saw that people in passing had stopped, had accumulated to a throng, to look at what had recently been a young woman, whose head was splattered on the pavement in red and orange, and who (whose corpse) just then he was passing very near. He turned away the moment he saw it, the shell of the recently deceased person (the fresh cadaver circled at a comfortable distance by the crowd of gapers). But while he felt nearly incapable of shock or surprise those days the scene lingered in his mind. Maybe because he'd never seen anything like that, because of the choking gray and the early hour, due to the canaille stopped staring blank-faced in their grotesque interest; because she'd fallen or jumped from one of the upper

130

floors of a hotel he'd lived in a few months before; because primary school students on their way to school might have witnessed the fall, and many would have seen the carnage in going to school (the body lay at the mouth of a lane that led to such an institution). And it was the day after Christmas. His own lifestyle was again increasingly dangerous and especially for this reason it made him consider how precious life was. [And in fact soon after—the predawn morning of January second—he was again confronted by gore when, while drunk, he discovered a man right outside the entrance of the bar he (the last patron, an inebriate in a merry mood) had just left at closing time, a man beaten within an inch of his life, his face mutilated, who bled on him when he knelt down to speak to him (a man he had in fact spoken to briefly an hour or two earlier); and he wept due to drunkenness, empathy, and horror to the night.] He'd just seen Hong Kong and felt he loved life, that all he wanted to do was live it. He'd started o-six with a bang, literally. He was in Guangzhou airport, people-watching, as he sat alone in one of a great many small waiting areas getting drunk from cans of beer. He was fucking an enthusiastic little nineteen-year-old again that night, he had a lot of crazy new stories, and he regarded himself as the most confident, truly adventurous, freest, coolest person alive and felt that amour-propre was good for him. Lately (because of all the pussy he was getting) he got erections very often, of priapismic duration. He loved flying, loved the dirty world and his place(s) in it; he was completely okay with what many might consider his moral corruptness—H.K. was a good place to live it up if you had some money. Life was fast then so fast. When his temper came out it rendered him monstrous, and when it rarely started ratcheting up he trembled uncontrollably, twitched like an epileptic prior to having a grand mal or like a malfunctioning android, and did whatever possible to stop that from happening. Presently, sitting there without a can of brew and having been downing them one after the other, he needed to piss and buy beer. Returned, back in Hangzhou, he sat in what was called simply Jazz Bar—having passed out on the plane home (on which a married older woman he woke to find seated beside him flirted with him, gave him her number), and having needed to urinate on the shuttle bus from the airport within minutes of getting on, the journey a blur—listening to someone named Katie Melua, who sang a fine rendition of "Blues in the Night." He'd had intercourse just minutes earlier with a different girl than he'd anticipated, a girl of eighteen who, unlike the one he had been looking forward to fucking again, didn't kiss his entire upper body and let him kiss hers nor lick inside his ears and suck on his lower lip while he was inside her but whom he did come inside a good deal, which was unspeakably satisfying (with the other he hadn't), and at times he thought brought near pain; and he ran his freezing hands across her back and stomach while she was on the phone with her boyfriend (she shuttered but her voice hardly faltered), and he remembered their mouths simultaneously open in ecstasy, her areolas and her small wet pussy neatly trimmed were mind-fresh, and he'd learned out of necessity to get off with a condom on (which was also good because the next time he could do without it would be pure bliss). And he was perhaps sexually obsessed and some would say awful, some evil, but what after

132

twenty-four women he really longed for was one once again who he could stay in all night and it was practically painful in more than one way to disconnect from, who totally wanted him, who got on top and moved in slow contentment (he thought of protuberant nipples, little details and small intimacies; of kissing a former lover from clavicle to chin, sucking on her earlobes. The grip of lower lips on his base and his engorged head probing deeply; feeling accepted, for the time, physically, totally). A woman who had three orgasms on his mouth or four on his cock.

In his head he was always repeating himself. He killed himself inexorably. Self-destruction was his modus operandi. A Chinese man sitting with three women (the trio pretty, in their thirties) just asked him to come over and toast them, which struck him as odd, despite his being a foreigner, because they weren't uncommon in Hangzhou. Maybe the guy had picked up on his good vibrations. He still had the sex flush. He'd been thirty thousand or so feet up a few hours earlier. She'd given Henry her number when he woke, the woman from the plane, an attractive lady. He was: a bruised specimen of possibility. A nether-being longing subconsciously for realms both infernal and ethereal. Too much, not enough, and nothing concrete. Even friends told him he was as an apple without a core, that he needed to get away from himself (he agreed at least with the latter appraisal but was quite attached—because he was incurably self-involved. He was also fairly not sane, generally speaking, speaking from self-knowledge). He sat next to a window in the dim café, watching people walk by. They let him drink unlimited beers until closing for thirty-seven RMB (all he had in his pocket);

he wasn't sure why. They made, he thought, an unwise decision, financially if in no other way. He devoured, and what any vice. He was an incorrigible virion, member of a species that was, behaviorally speaking, no different than a virus species; a long-surviving flea. He hated dumb attention as much as ass-kissing. He was not a zoo exhibit, at least till he found himself on Tralfamadore (was nothing but another slightly intelligent, slightly conscious human blob). The staring here (at the *lao wei*)...was silly, annoying. Unfortunately he'd recently eaten McDonald's two days in a row, each meal the price four or more would have been at most Chinese restaurants. At least he almost always ate the vastly healthier and better-tasting cuisine of the country he was in. In many ways he loved China, *Zhongguo*, totalitarian though it was. It was love-hate relationship, as it was with the Big Apple, a former home. He was sick of hearing "when I was in pigtails," however many a person was a two-face, and the train was a-callin'. Existence was a-callin', loudly and disturbingly. He'd been in some big towns, small towns, those in between. He was in Hangzhou—by any standard a big one—and hiccuping and thinking of how scary animate mannequins were, and it was one on the dot (by the clock visible from his spot). And he thought also about sheep-skin condoms and incredible dead people; about the utter meaninglessness of the larger part of human activity as documented, since there was no reason that perhaps even the whole of history was anything but (anything other than a record of follies; slow growth and quick extinctions; of facts, conqueror-composed, and associated dates) to those without God or a raison d'être, and that was why the concept of a celestial father figure appealed to

134

many—it kept despair at bay by making making life seem as though it wasn't pointless. And many needed or wanted a ruler too, a boss, whether a celestial or terrestrial one.

He was in such a sorry state, so he felt like walking strong on his way home. Nothing anymore stirred his soul, very rarely. He was diseased and without. He wound up on the sidewalk bleeding. Was life's opposite, a contradiction. The antithesis of the immensity...the all and the illusion, the sometimes-beautiful sometimes-terrible puzzle of no solution (while in the matrix) only attempted encapsulation, putting into words what was beyond vocabularies.

A different song was playing now. He heard *If you ain't coming with me gonna take somebody else*, the sound of a saxophone. For some reason he was thinking *Secondhand smoke murders babies*. Like Miss Melua, according to her lyrics, he didn't have anyone—just "reality." (He decided to hold his breath to rid himself of hiccups. A minute without oxygen never failed; sure enough it stopped the spasm.) One of the Chinese he drank with at the table he'd briefly gone over to was pretty hot. He sometimes found speaking Chinese slightly irritating, something about the sound of it partly. Sometimes he was sick of China, irked for example by the prostitute who asked "hao bu hao" or how to say breasts while he was clearly interested at the moment only in the part of the body of which she spoke, sick of feigned friendliness, and people bad with drink (who overdid it anyway), and (though it almost certainly applied more to his own nation) people who were kind of dense. ...And he generally disliked straight males who styled their hair, and people who thought they were intimidating on the basis of being drunk or spun, and people who thought they were tough because they worked out or wore oversized clothes and acted apelike; people who mistreated others for no reason, and foreigners who no matter what never ate the local cuisine (but instead subsisted exclusively on the less nutritious fare of their own hegemonic homeland), and people who were only technically adults though they were twenty-two.

————⟨◉⟩————

It was early evening on a Friday. A hardwood chair lay in the balcony sun, for reading, from which to watch the viewable world. (He liked the sun, Henry; it took his paleness. Most of his preadulthood he'd been pallid.) Unfortunately he had to keep the windows shut, as there were no screens, because of flying, biting things. Insects were an aspect of living in Asia that could not be ignored. The cockroaches though that he'd seen in China had as yet been small; gigantic mutant-like examples were not apparent, as they had been in Thailand (also absent were its tiny jingjos, pale lizards, which popped up in his room there and stealthily maneuvered on the walls until they escaped via the window)... He had a few beers, a lightning-fast shower, changed his garments... And later that night he watched guards in regimental green play a game of hoops versus blue-garbed Nike-outfitted men of the pedagogic profession on a half-court enclosed by a chain-link fence at a nearby "prisoner education" school; saw there sun-leathered resigned fiftysomething-year-old men raking grass clippings, the grass of the yards very green, seeming somehow sharply in contrast to the institution the greenery was on the grounds of, to the uniformed groups of players; had a feast of duck wing and pumpkin, chicken, bony fish, succulent beef, green vegetables and cow stomach soup with copious beer; and found himself on a maroon plush sofa in a darkened dance hall, first listening with half-feigned placidity to Chinese doing rounds of karaoke, then feeling himself become further attracted to the woman eight years his elder, a coworker, who sat beside him and was the only female he was ever around who spoke decent English (he wondered if he would find her better-looking with her glasses on or off, with or without lipstick, her bra strap visible or not)—and he didn't sing along or three-step so a different female colleague said, "I thought Americans were outgoing."

"Some."

"I thought most."

"Okay, many."

"Do you like being here?" she asked for the second time since they'd been speaking.

"Yes," he said, adding again, "It's fine...I'm used to places like this." *I'm more used to clubs. Which I also dislike*, he thought.

Seemingly to her annoyance he inquired about beer.

"This is a dance hall. You're not allowed to drink in here. Go to a bar."

"Then why is there a fridge full of beer outside the door?" he felt like asking but didn't, instead going back to reading, reading a book about China, a book he'd read the better part of before he'd arrived or knew he'd be coming.

Beer came soon, plenty of it. He ended up riding home on the back of a half-drunk male colleague's motorbike, without a helmet. It reminded him of bygone days not so long ago and he felt fleetingly alive. Before he'd left the restaurant at which he'd imbibed he was talking again to his female colleague who was a bitch and she had said, "You can't be older than twenty-three; you look too young."

"I'm twenty-four," he said, which he was in that place, where one's one at birth, and she said "I don't believe you," and for the third time said "You're way too young," and he too was half-drunk and was thinking that he could be categorized as antisocietal.

"You know riding a motorcycle without a helmet is very dangerous" he'd said to the closest thing he had to a friend in Hangzhou, the only same-gender coworker who spoke English with enough competency to meaningfully communicate with, as he watched the others, headgear-less all, depart on their motorbikes, merging with the chaotic flow of traffic, some with their young child seated behind them, women in the dresses they wore every day, men probably in the same shirts and slacks.

...Back out for beer and spiced goat on sticks and when he returned he paced and talked to himself, his soliloquy strange, and on eventually opening his nth bottle it shattered on the floor, pieces of green glass flying all the way across the room, beer flowing under his bed ("I guess it happens," he thought aloud, semi-audibly and as if given up). "Great. Fucking perfect. This is terrific," et cetera, he said (though not upset) as he picked up little pieces of bottle from the floor thinking how easy it would be for the soles of his feet to be embedded with unseen particles of glass, and sure enough he stepped on a few but they failed to puncture and he removed them gingerly (considering) from the yellow beds of his feet putting them in the wastebasket and mopped up the visible brew with a bright yellow towel thinking *This is my created life*, and unsurprising to Henry he was willful enough, though it was an ordeal (due to distance), to go out and buy a replacement, for which for being a foreigner he was overcharged by the boisterous and sturdy female shopkeeper, who was playing cards with three army guys, though he relented quickly, against principle, paying the price she told him, because the difference was the equivalent of six cents.

———— ((●)) ————

Henry, like most, speculated about the future, never experienced but as the present (in which the quality of the choices made determined—other than celestial/Earth events unalterable—the present to be. (A presiding death drive resulted in a future suffused with death/deathliness)). He thought that in the near future not enough—not by far—would yet have woken, no longer fooled, feeling stifled, and be making true strides against a zeitgeist of ignorance-hypocrisy-insanity; that the malaise of purposelessness, helplessness, an era of sedentary lives misspent in front of screens, of laziness, apathy, of tyrants, organizations and individuals, public and private, would go on. Infantilized serfs/subjects would be played like fiddles and daily stupefied, as they had been; the most powerful would generally continue to be as evil, to have as much power, as ever. Even a mass movement—which was incredibly unlikely—would be met with mass suppression. The destruction would not be abated, the stream of lies would stay undammed, the rivers would by and large remain the opposite. The tides would not change; world powers would. Policies would be altered only to be more fascist, to give plebs less wiggle room under the jackboot. Instead of the Federal Reserve being abolished and defense/military/(illegal) war spending being substantially decreased, instead of everyone being provided costless health care and a college education (if not food and housing), rather than economic slaves becoming a thing of the past, what could and should be (which would be much too much positive progress given the direction, state of the State. Progress that, if it did occur, would be—like the governmental response to climate change—late and slow).

The warming of the planet would make the weather more severe, erratic, the world more unpleasant and difficult to inhabit. Legislative changes, coming about at a snail's pace, would hardly make a difference (in twenty-twelve there would be a disaster (among many), a continuing ecological one, along with which the socioeconomic state of affairs would continue as it had for so long to not be what it should). The government, big interests, big agendas, big media would generally win—over the always expanding and consuming mass, a mass that despite ever diminishing resources, new diseases, bacteria, and the flourishing, the ubiquity of some existing ones would keep growing, a virus itself, a horde among which, as historically, those with wealth weathered best the ongoing grand storm.

Or, given what seemed an essentially accurate conclusion

140

about the character of the true directors of America (super-corporation going under) based on the record of the past, and given that one of the big agendas of those few at the peak of the pyramid of international power was a massive—more so than would be necessary to achieve their (other) goals without hindrance from the public—population die-off, maybe a virus, a syndrome, would be manufactured (or maybe it wouldn't need to be) that successfully exterminated or enfeebled the mass of the mass, the mainly uneducated many; alternatively bellicose bigwigs and banker-funded puppets would get a good war started (in which nuclear and/or chemical and/or biological weapons were used) that did the job (likely—desirably—killing a lot of people from around the globe), while those running the show as usual held on to their health in hidden or well-guarded places (the people with money, which was power, or with power besides faring best—eating caviar, crumpets and jam, drinking wine and espresso, their crops growing underground; though least deserving of life living materially the best; dwelling in lairs more immense than the largest city, quadruple-reinforced with the strongest material economically feasible and very deep—as the world, metaphorically or literally, burned). As long as the population remained on the rise though—while the swine were permitted to copulate with a choice of mates, wallow in their pens, and swill their swill—promiscuity, callousness, and amorality would intensify, increase; attention spans decrease, happiness become ever more evanescent, illusory.

He wished having the money to meet his needs did not entail a loss of freedom, that he were not tied (by himself, of necessity) to, seemingly dependent on his inane and even evil job as a minimum-wage minion—a poller: a sad, soul-sapping non-career that required him to spout the same shit on different days (that came to feel the same) to the same types (he sat in a cubicle-filled artificially cool and lit building and soon after his shift began had zoned out, as was his wont), to read propaganda (primarily to people who already believed it) written by entities associated with the not-new regime. At this job he mostly despised he sat for the duration a few inches from a radiation-emitting buzzing black screen (the monitor an old, graffitied one) in a drab two-story structure, and the performance of his duties didn't require him to do much thinking, not recently. On occasion he couldn't *make* himself focus on the words that were coming out of his mouth he had uttered them so many times or they were so well known to be b.s. (but if he was too fucked up to say the words correctly and in the right sequence then he was fucked); in fact he came to know the database, the survey formats, the nature of the polls the company did so well, could conduct them so robotically—and the more automaton-like he was in doing his job the more satisfactory a job he was considered to be doing, by those above him whose task it was to assure quality for the nefarious ones above them—that he could perform his duty there practically brainlessly (as was to his thinking ideal, providing he expended mental power

142

during his time calling the anonymous public on something that required it, and was worthwhile).

He thought back to the job of the same sort that had been a prelude to the one less strict but in significant ways worse that he would hold much longer.

"Given the gambling aspect of the sport, how acceptable is it for a company to sponsor horse racing?" read a question in the main poll he conducted when he had his first telephone research position.

"Which soft drink company sponsors your local or the nearest NFL team?" read another.

It was because of that job, that survey, that he gained the useless knowledge that Major League Baseball had an official cheese-filled snack sponsor.

He remembered it had been there, within the no longer utilized building where he was initially introduced to the world of over-the-phone data collection/marketing/propagandizing, that he first spoke the ten words he would later say by rote countless times to innumerable faceless individuals: "Very, somewhat, a little bit, or not at all interested?"

He'd conducted the same poll each day at that call center (though not necessarily for the entirety of every shift)—sports survey, as it had been unimaginatively dubbed. The sports survey family they'd called themselves, his fellow drones of various ages, sizes and personalities (few of whom he spoke with—and none of whom he spoke to frequently. Instead (during breaks, before and after he clocked in, when socializing was allowed) he preferred to stand alone—gaunt and cross-looking, smoking—stoic or feeling he was; preferred to stand staring absently at a hedge, or a wall, at stucco or plaster; at a fenced garden across the street, someone's recently ejected or now-petrified snot and/or spit: scenery which was inanimate, disinteresting, about which he experienced no conscious thoughts or feelings, only the lack thereof) who spent the better part of each workday saying the same sentences, perhaps twenty minutes' worth of them, to different people.

———◦(◊)◦———

He considered the system—within which he was a number, a statistic, a slave or unhelpful to it, disposable in either case—unjust, a farce, meant to consolidate and maintain the power, preserve its own structure. A system of the disingenuous, by design economically inequitable, that failed slowly as more average people became impoverished (though its failure was perhaps part of a master plan). He reflected on a Supreme Court justice ruling for mandatory microchips under American skin, a judge of the court that earlier overrode democracy to install the most destructive president in the nation's history. Mercenaries stalking the Big Easy and, dressed as Arabs to provoke tribal conflict, Iraq. Glaciers melting and the acidification of the rising brine; the Patriot Act and the big lie that paved the way for it and another two imperialistic wars plus a war, exactly Orwellian, of indefinite duration against...a word (a word for what the U.S. and its people—and other countries and other peoples, many more, financial terrorism included—had been and was still being subjected to). Thought about how the nations of the world were each year more corporatized, connected—as debt ate America like necrotizing fasciitis. And needless dead were filed away. Dead, deader than the dead walking (any of whom could see martial law, detention in a FEMA facility, World War III), that'd been riders on the storm. Considered the fact that every U.S. citizen had many a number attached to them (all having been born into the system)—and records, files (anonymity, privacy was a past privilege). And multitudinous were those who been filed away though yet breathed, some of whom still raised their ruddy faces to the clouds, shook their fists at the heavens, screamed "I'm mad as hell" out their windows.

————※⟨●⟩※————

It was February. He was at a tavern, leaning against the bar. "What've you been doing?" asked an acquaintance.

He shrugged. "Fucking life." He took a drink from his beer.

We are all just organisms, he thought. He sometimes imagined a sort of misery, excruciating—sometimes of the kind that would bring him to the threshold of death, bodily and otherwise—that horrified though would probably never be experienced by him (or at least so he hoped). Pictured his Achilles' heels being slashed, pictured himself being forced to ingest nonedibles, saw the insertion of objects, the injection of foreign liquids; imagined being burned, cut up; being restrained, confined, tortured any number of ways—by instruments and acid, by sleep-deprivation or blaring music

145

and white lights. Saw himself being held in a small damp black chamber and given only food enough to starve very gradual; being used Mengele-style by sadist or psycho.

⸺◈⸺

It was nine-twenty and he was well upon the drunk train, the one that never left without him. Currently, it wasn't sex that he wanted, it was something more expensive and harder to come by. Reciprocal affection, and mutual understanding, mutual acceptance, and what ingredients were necessary for the idea of love. The ideal. No matter how much time one spent in Netherland, on the couch or pavement, they could still be a romantic in this way and in the grand tradition of seeking the feeling of freedom (in the sense of carefreeness, letting loose—or never really getting hold), adventure.

He'd just bought five more beers, and some packaged preservative-filled goat meat on sticks, spicy, greasy and delicious, and there were some rotting apples in the fridge should he want to eat more and maybe get drunker (though he thought finishing all the beer he now possessed that night—because of how soused he already was—would mean bad times for him). By Chinese standards he had a shit-load of cash (no, was well above the poverty threshold). He thought: I'm a fucking pimp. Hard-used Shitstank, USA, is doing alright. Must keep on keeping on; reading on; seeking out. It felt like he was going to be in his twenties forever. No matter, age, all, was illusory. Presently he wished he could jump through his silly, singular life to some better point that contained more simple sense. Mind meandering, he considered that, as drunkard, he had averted, caused and circumvented some minor fiascoes.

———((●))———

In his sight were many primates. Drunken monkeys in bars looking at girls' asses as they passed, as they bent over playing pool. And he from some corner, in the dark at a remove, was watching the beasts, observing them hatefully, fucked up though he was too. Appreciating the same sights as they were, but substantially less obviously, more on his mind at any given moment he suspected than was on any of theirs over a string of seconds (seconds that for eternity had been spent among the other scarcely visible inebriated predators, bipedal desire-driven stars of their own unimportant and largely uninteresting movies).

———((●))———

For the first time in memory he'd discovered he had two concurrently open beers. Such slips happened with near-constant alcohol consumption. When one was in psychic disrepair. (He knew he needed to stop drinking like he was—a beer necessary immediately in the morning, his workplace desk drawer full of empty beer cans, room full of empty green bottles—but no. He wanted to leave China but wanted to stay; wanted to leave Earth but wanted to stay...)

147

Halloween was the next day. All Hallows' Eve. The day it was the eve of had been established by invading Roman Catholics to discourage druidic ceremonies for the god of darkness on the previous day, but with the increasing popularity of witchcraft the ritual grew instead, more to the Catholics' displeasure, and in mockery of them the day of these ceremonies was renamed All Hallows' Eve. To Henry the creepiest Halloween costume would be Punchinello (which reminded him of the Martin-Lewis tune, the last song in their last movie, seen in childhood); stylized Punchinello/ Pulcinella costumes were particularly spooky-looking, the character seeming malicious and inhuman, to him.

All cities began to look the same he'd heard it said (and he agreed) once you'd seen enough of them, but bare breasts never seemed to; they were typically sightly (before they started to wither). He hadn't been laid since being out of America yet felt he missed unclothed tits even more than vaginas; they made the best pillows (even over goose feathers). Nipples were nice. There were various kinds of those too. He knew a girl once who had the most protuberant ones, and they were very sensitive. She was eighteen, and Chinese-American, and on a golf course in daylight, he sitting on a boulder as she knelt between his legs, he taught her fellatio using an ice cream cone analogy.

Some of the pornographic DVDs (illegal) in China were hodgepodges of random material of the sort that sometimes included bestiality and hardcore bondage, and though he had no particular issue with viewing either the former he found unerotic if not boring, but the other interesting because the specifics of the degradation the women volunteer for are in

148

some cases supposedly unknown to them beforehand, the (again supposed) interview where they do so being occasionally included. And the administrant of torment is probably a psychopath (or gives that impression) and he informs them preliminarily that his aim is pain not pleasure. And the women are not porn star quality and have perhaps cigarette burns and cellulite, maybe scars from old slashes self-inflicted, and had bad childhoods, and their mammary glands are revealed, remarkable in regularity, by scissor through cheap blouse. They are teary-, feary-eyed and confused (it seems when the hoods they wear at first are removed) because they've been bound and contorted by so many ropes and chains by a hirsute black-clad master, and he presses his erection-less groin into mascara-run faces and asks what they would do to stop the pain (to be released from the forced poses, for the circulation to be restored to various parts of their bodies). Lifted up, tightly restrained, via pulleys—snot-strings hanging from faces flushed and upside-down—they are expectorated on, slapped, perhaps pinched or peed on; and when it is over they have a little cash, bite marks, friction burns and nothing. They are spit and shit and at some point they probably got off on it.

<hr />

A few years after graduating high school he was residing and working shitty jobs in the same general area he'd grown up in. Hanging out at his one-time dealer's house taking rips off the pipe going round and watching teenage girls lie on

149

the living room carpet and watch their mind-numbed boy-friends sit playing *Halo* or *Gran Turismo*; and spending time at more discomforting houses, houses the outside and inside and minds of the occupants of which were becoming dilapidated with slug-slowness. Snorting white drugs then being up for forty-eight hours even after drinking twenty-four beers; attending untold parties at which beer and twenty-something strangers (abrasive, boring, attractive, incomprehensible, inaccessible) were in abundance.

It seemed as if his memory could always yield interactions that were disappointing; sex that was not fully satisfying, that was sometimes awkward, or left him futilely wanting more, either with the same person or in general. Alcohol-intensified desolation, alcohol-induced erraticism; recollections of vomiting or throwing things in or getting eightysixed from bars, living in very small or stark rooms, becoming catatonic or impertinent in public settings, passing out anywhere conceivable...scenes from a nightmare (epic, endless-seeming).

———— «◉» ————

(Though he regarded it a minor issue, he was depressed, as always—no, as usual. Any means of getting out of and preventing the recurrence of his depression eluded him. It had gone on so long. He felt purposeless, without ambition, practically nonextant, considered himself an introverted cipher—young but no less inscrutable. There was only distraction, what passed for fleeting happiness. He knew already that life was meaningless misery and then it ended—or so was his acquired outlook—but this knowledge, perhaps unsurprisingly, made living no less painful. He required an outlet and he had one, so he had only to endure, the alternative to which was to die. He was an ant doing Earth-time, time in the ant-farm, the many ants going to and fro about their silly business—he no better or worse than any of them; unique like them all; of no more consequence than any. To this one everything seemed prematurely dead; he thought of one's future moment of demise as being no different from any other moment—they were one. For him the past was torturous. The present was merely an ordeal, though not actually palpable, less real than the future even. If the present was as real as either past or future he felt he could hold on to it, that maybe he could stop time (probably choosing the peak of a really great orgasm). ...No. No, on second thought the past was unreal, as was the future; the only reality was the evanescent present. And in the present there were always choices that could have a more or less positive effect on one's future.)

He was covertly drinking a can of beer in his office, an office shared by a number of occupational equals. There was nothing to do but drink his brew (well, that wasn't quite true). He was thinking: even more than he felt the need for catharsis he felt the need for love. He was just so goddamn doomed. And longing. Pathetically, self-sickeningly. And complicated, even to himself. And worthless-feeling (like a fucked guy no one ever wanted to fuck), troubled. Below the surface self-loathing. Why did he even bother? he asked himself. He thought: If I could smoke a j right now none of anything would matter at all.

He was doing coke not infrequently when he was in Oregon last and he'd do more of that. Yes, he wanted to do more drugs he was thinking the previous night. Especially shrooms and acid (too bad the latter was especially hard for him to obtain); but weed first and foremost, weed was all he would ever need. Shit I need some weed, he thought. Here he was going off the deep end. But he couldn't, there was no deep end really. (Or if there was he had long ago reached it.) The only real end was to throw himself from the fourth story (or perhaps a prison term, especially a substantial one). But he'd never do it. He'd never do it, though he thought about such actions often enough, for one reason because he wasn't that much of a pussy, too pussy for life, or was too pussy to ruin his body and bring to an end his life.

He'd had a runny nose all week but not a cold. Infrequently he'd catch coryza but his system would flush it out in a day. A Chinese pop song blasted from the speakers. It was not his limited Mandarin that told him it was about love. He'd come to experience here a strong sensation of isolation. He could watch every American movie on the internet about as soon as it came out stateside; that kept him somewhat occupied. He was also exercising more than he ever had in lieu of drinking fiendishly, which was mostly how he'd spent his free time until recently. There were though recent enough drunken escapades. Due to inebriation he seemed to've broken a toe the night before he mounted the Great Wall, which he only walked along for ninety minutes (it was a bit painful and it was a clear late morning and he'd started from the most touristy entrance, in Badaling near Beijing). It suddenly smelled of farts in his office, unexplainably. He was drinking a Pepsi and smoking Ma Fei (flying horse) cigarettes—the cheapest ones, the equivalent of about thirteen cents per pack. He kept dreaming in pornography (or having dreams that incorporated sex), or about being in strange settings and feeling disoriented, or death-like.

⟺⟨●⟩⟺

His present residence, a studio apartment—in general on the substandard side (a trend in China); nothing in it functioned initially—had a water cooler, a big TV that was only good for watching static, and a big fridge and small microwave neither of which he had use for; had hygiene and especially beauty products, a bag of salt, and a quarter bottle of wine left by the prior occupant; a bathroom, actually a wetroom, with a urinal in addition to a toilet (operated by manually lifting the plug in the tank, the bowl waterless); a water heater that was capable only of rendering water lukewarm, and two sinks: one flat and designed for washing clothes, the other deep, the dirty map inside it when he moved in still untouched.

In the People's Republic occupying quite a lot of space and numerous types of terrain were quite a lot of people (and thus a lot of taxis, and bikes like the one that once in an

153

incautious moment laid him out briefly, causing him to bite his tongue), the varied (but mostly Han) inhabitants of a large country with a long history—dynasty after dynasty, invasion upon invasion—and accordingly a richness of culture. The cuisine was diverse too—and one expression of Chinese hospitality was to serve more than could be eaten—much of it peculiar, such as dog, consumed in some places (he'd never had the opportunity to try it had he been so inclined; however, he had sampled snake in snake blood soup, frog, fragrant pig intestine, and bean curd—tofu that tasted, he thought, more like feces must than the intestine, which probably contained traces of excrement, had and was in fact quite popular). Common were sweet lotus root soup, and pea popsicles; fat rather than meat and meat—though you teeth-shatteringly might think otherwise!—that was mostly bone (most meat served contained bones, which you spat onto your plate or the table).

Chinese were, generally, big spitters; one would often see someone hawking a loogie, or blowing their nose onto the ground. See, sometimes, naked babies; sometimes, in rural areas, naked babies shitting on the sidewalk. Tea was omnipresent, everyone drank it. And there was a high ratio of smokers and beer-drinkers, and good-looking women who more likely than their Thai counterparts would give you a dirty look if you even made eye contact (or didn't), and sometimes (when they smiled, spoke, et cetera) revealed tooth-rot, which was very prevalent—primarily, he believed, because the water was dirty, nonpotable.

A wide selection of pirated DVDs, CDs, and poor quality practically anything could be found easily and for a low price. The economy was growing at a fast clip and as it did materialism and the popularity of Western culture were on the upswing. Walking, you'd see a lot of pink-lit massage parlors that typically offered extra services. Be able to watch someone getting a filling through the large window of a dentist's office as if the attention of interested persons was desired. TV soap operas were big; to play and watch so was table tennis, badminton also; and basketball, Yao Ming of course being very popular. And a news program on state TV would tell you about a traffic accident and then show you a guy in the hospital with a hole in his abdomen and if he was conscious a reporter would put a microphone in his face and ask something like "How's it feel to have your intestines falling out?" and he'd answer as calmly and politely as possible.

Social boundaries were fewer and less restrictive; the lack of privacy pervasive—which made sense in a way considering the size of the populace. The traffic was treacherous and people were frequently hit (though China had citizens to spare. During the Cultural Revolution people were told to breed like bunnies—after which, boom! there was a population problem, and they were limited to a single child per couple, probably for the best). There was, not surprisingly, a lot of mistranslation, on signs, labels, many things that— especially in a more developed province like Zhejiang, the one he currently resided in—were written in English as well. It was occasionally funny, other times confusing, misleading, even stupefying. But the English was, while usually syntactically wrong, helpful since he couldn't read Chinese, or really speak it (he could count to nine hundred-ninety-nine. He also knew *lao wei* and *Meiguo ren*, 'foreigner' and 'American', because they were his names, and being a *Meiguo ren* often gave him a twinge of displeasure because he felt there was a connotation attached, a bundle of assumptions (for one there was no convincing them he wasn't well-off) like a piece of muslin through which he was unjustly, inaccurately seen. That 'American' was a descriptor that rendered him in the minds of most Chinese a thing—rather than a person, individual; the kind of guy for example who less than a week earlier was getting drunk solitarily, but in style, in the dining car of an express sleeper train on the thirteen-hour trip from Beijing to Hangzhou, who took pride in such memories).

⸺◦«◉»◦⸺

The power had recently gone out for some portion of the medium-size city (he'd been in the midst of masturbating to *Caligula* when the place went black). Presently he was pissing in the back of an internet café upon a large fresh turd it pained him to think may have come out of a female, thinking, as he sometimes would childishly, nonseriously, that his urine stream by hitting it somehow connected it with his body, created a germ passage. He returned home considering that he'd had no sleep the prior night; despite that in his third wind he wasn't feeling tired but was only happily lucid—probably because he lapsed into an unexpected couch nap of an hour and a half, from nine-ish to ten-thirty—and only at six forty-five did he sense much chance of getting more slumber (though when that occurred he was pretty wrapped up in *Melinda and Melinda*, in which Will Ferrell, essentially doing Woody Allen, was delightful).

The next morning, still needing to catch up on sleep, he had half-awake hallucinations of a haunting sort, still sofa-situated with a quilt (the sun bright, filling the room, rendering it eye-paining yellow), and chirpbirds, children noises and barks, bumps, knocks, slams (and adults going to work and pruney women on their way to exercise in the stone courtyard to bad techno and sometimes employing jump ropes)—these sounds of China waking early on time kept rousing him, morn cruelty, jarring him from continued peace no matter how brief it would have been (though maybe for the best, as he was able to shower, brush and dress, flag a cab (he'd reacquired the habit of wasting money on taxis; and also of sometimes using dumbbells in an ever-ongoing albeit irregularly fought battle against the encroach of physical weakness), with time to spare—and the work morning flowed into the past without incident and he even displayed uncharacteristic zeal. Yes, he in fact operated like a fine-tuned robot in sleep-deprived bliss, though was hardly managing to keep one eye open even to scale stairs before his appearance at work).

Later, he was halfway through a bottle of beer ordered on finding himself in a dim restaurant—dim though it was a pleasant enough April afternoon, and the glass front doors were wide, and the windows were wide and without blinds or curtains—having drained the can he aimlessly plodded the street with (which he'd still been killing off, king drunk, on entrance) while unconsciously devising some palpable void activity following his discovery of an unknown section of the city that was operating as if stuck in an earlier age (something that was not uncommon) and speculating what the underpaid blue-uniformed hard laborers hammering with steel sporadic clinks partly obscured in a concrete pit in the farthest traffic lane were working on (their presence was, he decided, related to the power outage), and on the table was a lighter he'd just procured, and it was wrapped with a print of a Chinese girl with monstrous breasts (rare, but he'd had such a woman).

———=◦《◉》◦=———

There was an elderly man on TV talking about World War II and a small garden out the window on the right with grapes of both colors dripping from its roof. And before him there was a lit cigarette, an open beer, and an effeminate Chinese pop star seemed to stare sideways at him from his also table-situated water bottle, the atoms of which were in flux (on the molecular level unseen operations often taken for granted were occurring uninterruptedly).

Out in public there were a lot of sexually attractive women. It was frustrating because the only realistic way he knew of getting laid was paying for the services of a prostitute, and he felt he really oughtn't press his, to him incredible, luck (not to have contracted an STD) anymore with ventures of such a sort. (Nearly two months and he could only look, and self-satisfy.)

Now the cigarette was gone and the beer empty and he contemplated purchasing a third bottle (very cheap but merely three-point-six percent). It was six-thirty or so.

He thought of the tirade scene in *25th Hour* as he thought:

Fuck: stupid fucking people (there were so many, among Americans, and they were so awful); gangsta wannabe motherfuckers and their hos (especially white ones, but all posers—who seemed to usually wear hats); fucking yuppies with no hair out of place (or so they would prefer), with a mobile phone that never leaves their hand; guys who care about being tough, who act like they are or want to be what they think that means; beggars who think or act as if you owe them something; any sound-bodied so-called man (or woman) who (when he/she had no more right to a given trajectory than Henry) he ever moved for rather than they for him; jocks and sports obsessees; women who dress like tramps and when you look at them they glare; thug pretenders (aforecited), evangelical Christians, Republicans (Democrats too; members of both puppet-propping supposedly distinct primary parties (two heads of one serpent), the campaigns of the status quo-maintaining presidential candidates of which were corporately financed—meaning that if/when they took office they were in the corporations' pockets for the entirety of their terms, were the highest ranking agents of the corporatocracy), and anyone who didn't see the link between CO_2 emissions since the Industrial Revolution and ongoing and worsening climate change, who didn't give a shit about the environment or see that humans had recently and drastically altered it (and serious consequences for them were already occurring).

———⟨◉⟩———

August fifth: Typhoon Matsa struck at night, throwing tree limbs and destroying the umbrella of anyone unfortunate enough to be out when it got going. Through tea-rowed mountains, steppes and road construction, hot asphalt and hot sun, he'd arrived sleepy, bumpily, in the "small" city he was presently inhabiting (Wenling). Out his hotel window he had a perfect view of a restaurant across the street, Mi Bao Wan. Loud Chinese with their brews and foods sat at or were congregated around the outdoor tables, laughing over the music, the din, and getting louder each hour; Fengyuanchaoshi, a supermarket, adjacent, its sign also brightly glowing.

Here he was always grabbing the A.C. remote when he wanted the TV remote; in the tub with no curtain (but at least a tub) always mistaking the foam bath, which he never used anyway, for the shampoo—the last time even putting it in his hair. He should have remembered after how long it'd been the shampoo was the blue one (or remembered to just throw the other bottle away), and probably would in the future, but nevertheless he felt his mind was going, had been going (people's minds were always going after a point, even as they were in ways improving), and he, with his continued formidable alcoholism, his past of this and drug use/abuse, was helping it along.

Henry walked in the sun so much on a regular basis

(the sun that glared currently through a partly open curtain, strange close star making possible puny everyone's existences) that he had a farmer's tan—soldier's tan as an Israeli guy of his brief acquaintance had called it.

At home, at the Ching Ma (gold horse) Hotel, he absentmindedly almost squeezed liquid seasoning into the ashtray with the lit cigarette in it instead of into the plastic container of noodles he was boiling water for, which was also on the bed. Ping-pong was on, China v. Korea, a doubles game, China up. He wasn't actually watching but reading and slowly drinking a Pepsi, on its blue label beside the widely recognizable logo the upper body and airbrushed visage of another or the same effeminate pop star that he'd previously seen on a bottle of water.

━━●))━━

He needed to sleep but hadn't started to wind down yet. He was watching the national news, CCTV (China Central Television). Big-mustachioed Bolton, newly confirmed, had just been on briefly. America can go fuck itself, he thought, already has. He lately was trying to learn Mandarin to a conversational degree (a difficult tongue) and, he reminded himself, an alcoholic who'd been drinking to the point it'd become economically straining. Was at present in a so-called small town of five to seven hundred thousand. Near the East China Sea apparently. At present was recollecting that his vomiting alter ego had been released one night by too much harsh Chinese whiskey quickly consumed (so that other was quickly released); being accosted by a prostitute in Shanghai the first night he was in the country and nearly hit by a car, sleek, dark-colored and new, on escaping her, she who had unyieldingly chosen him (though it was supposed to work the other way); the Kansas girl of shoulder-length blonde hair, light freckle cheeks and no little sex appeal whom he made out with also the first night never to see again, a young healthy woman of classic Midwestern beauty. Was experiencing ennui and insomnia. Sometimes he woke and didn't want to be alive and he wondered *Will that change?*

Sometimes he had to avert his eyes until his darkness went (first Henry's darkness grew but then it went), his mind, like a creature of habit, eventually returning to the dark (where it would occasionally linger—as if taking in the sights and smells of a physical realm—whether or not by his volition, which it usually was not).

⸻ ((◦)) ⸻

He remembered he used to feel terrible all over his body. Briefly, unexpectedly, inexplicably. The sensation seemed to emanate from his crotch as if a symptom of a long undiagnosed sexually contracted disease. He had stopped experiencing it, those days had gone, but he didn't know that it wouldn't return. (He also didn't know for certain that it (like so much else) hadn't been psychologically manufactured.) It reminded him of a terrible itching rash he'd developed in Southeast Asia—where, in some places, such afflictions (the origins of which might forever be mysterious, but were usually environmental conditions) were common—a rash that had flared up at times, though thankfully went away not long after he returned to the States.

———)(◉)(———

Henry's girlfriend, whom he felt he was in love with, was to return over the weekend. When she did he wanted to lay with and caress her in the grass of the nearby park, supplied with whiskey so he didn't have to piss every half-hour. One drawback to constant beer consumption was peeing all the time; liver damage, applicable to that level of alcohol ingestion in general, was another downside. Which reminded him they were to go to the hospital, she to translate, so he could finally receive a verdict on whether or not said organ, often aching, had already become seriously deteriorated. And she'd buy food and cook as usual, help him get a decent haircut. Then later they would come together—would have their intercourse, ideal, a reminder that sex could be spiritual, and that that was the highest wish one could have for it.

He was awfully far gone and considering not going back immediately after his contract ended, no matter how it went with his lady friend, but was aware it was partly out of his hands. He thought about her constantly, and had dreams about her—troubled dreams, of troubling things that were not her fault. Yet it was not her that tempted him, if he might even be able, to remain in the country—more so it was his vision of the America from which he'd departed, of another long sentence of griping drudgery. It was not alcoholism,

163

for there it would undoubtedly not be severe, but the fear of known horrors and casualties of expectation.

The girl on his lighter didn't have particularly outstanding breasts, not large ones anyway, she was just squeezing them together. His father used to love a certain soap opera that aired afternoons, afternoons its being on seemed to render dull. He learned from an episode he once saw of a prime time newsmagazine that there were women who saved and (as the goat and hare) ate their own placentas, or sold them to people who ate placentas; that they were a fine source of nutrients, and that their consumption was supposed to preclude postpartum depression and increase milk production.

═══━━◄(●)►━━═══

Days he forgot about were when he casually and causally threw up undigested noodles all over the street and viewed *Once Upon a Time in America* starting at midnight, after passing out. Days he spoke lines from favorite action films to fictitious foes in imaginary reality-informed scenarios. Days he managed reasonable conversation in Mandarin and the legs of a nothing-special, even unattractive middleaged woman who ran a shop he was buying beer from were on display to him while leisurely she picked the jam from between her toes and asked "Xiao jiu gui, dui bu dui?" and he said "Dui." When his right thumb was slightly bruised from having broken an aluminum bar into five pieces the night before in idleness while intermittently blacked out. He'd recently discovered, recalled, a freckle on his lower thorax.

164

Afternoon, in especially inebriated haze—the old men and their bloated wives passed in gray and streak, chewing their gums and strolling placidly. He made eyes at numerous ripe females who typically were unaware, who otherwise were alarmed by his appearance, reciprocal, offered learned dead stares. A man on an unmoving motorbike steadied a foot in a worn brown shoe against a short tree and held his arms behind his head relaxing in the recent heat. A hoary fellow sat on the other side of this tree, in a pedicab, watching the world with less interest than Henry was—for it again unfolded and he knew such elaborate thoughts, fancies, fun delusions. He was in that fickle moment. He was, during his nap, bitten by an exceedingly small mosquito, three times. Flies buzzed in the yellow swarm of life outside the doors and devotchkas were beginning to rely more on skirts. There were, always, so many pieces of day it was impossible to recall or fully comprehend them (as with others aware of the vastness and their inability to process what they cannot know, whose existences weren't dull, due to their degree of consciousness).

He'd sent an email to a girlfriend past, a girl a few years his junior who was never actually his girlfriend, saying her bra no longer smelled like her and asking if he could loan it to her to wear for a while. Sometimes, quite drunk, he sent messages like this to female friends or acquaintances but they eventually reacknowledged him anyway, to some degree knowing he was sick (in ways plural was he ill).

His present girlfriend was great at sucking cock and held his dick as they slept, one time with her lips all half-dream early morning. Prior to his leaving for work they typically

165

made love, though this meant he had to worry about getting erections throughout the day and knowing he smelled slightly of pussy (because they'd often not finish until five, ten minutes before he had to be out the door).

Dreams invaded "reality" and he had trouble distinguishing the difference. His formerly broken fingers and toes had of late begun to ache.

(So it seemed, or so he'd convinced himself. Maybe they were one; maybe it was all the injuries that evoked in his mind the image of a superficially broken and naturally fused man.)

—————◄((●))►—————

It happened that the seed of the desire to do people harm had been sown or come into existence in Henry; it was not there or he was not aware of it until he was twenty-one, during which year his life became particularly shitty, because of being he felt generally mistreated by society (when Henry remembered the period and certain incidents he was filled with a warm hate), because of frustration, because of his undeserved station, torments. It was hate that reminded him to finally get an STD check—and if he, say, had HIV he would be sure to inflict his wrath on society (and do so without it mattering) before he went.

In some Mideastern countries young girls were married to full-grown men; in some Islamic states women wore contourless clothes and left only eyes exposed, so that their bodies did not trigger so-called impure thoughts in men's minds. All were animals, every human example; capable of, genetically wired for, violence. Everyone could be evil (except perhaps literal morons). Some were to various extents in general; practically all were at one time or another. One person might be more evil than another, might have thoughts another didn't, might act upon what many others wouldn't. Always there had been such people, those more on the maleficent side, and maybe always there would be, and now there were no doubt more than there'd ever been. Henry was not a good example of an evil or demented specimen. But a part of him (his mind) was or had been something similar (or exactly that) sometimes before, to a degree—a part that could have caused more havoc if not for the problem of consequence, potentially quite the specter.

People were nature and nurture, like similar primates only at a higher level of development. To live was to die, but energy could not be destroyed any more than a lifetime could be unlived.

------------◦((◦))◦------------

He was at a club (which, by virtue of being a club, reminded Henry of Thailand in a way that was probably more negative than positive—of unrequited lust (and here, presently, he was conscious of his desire for a perfect-looking about thirty-year-old Chinese woman that his colleague, yet another molded-haired striped-dress-shirt-clad douche, had somehow managed to acquire), of blaring, penetrating techno, of retreating into himself and staring at no one and nothing in particular; a wall, someone's patinaed hair, unconsciously)—where makeuped women in iridescent blouses moved to a steady stentorian pulse and people of both genders were meat-hunting; where young men with gelled hair and sharp shirts came up to desirable females dancing alone with whom they mimicked sex to music in semi-darkness, in very close proximity but infrequently touching. Where over a large area of particolored floor there were mated dancers, happy, healthy, perfumed, in their twenties; where among tables and drinks, erratic beams that lit at random strangers' faces, teeth, shoulders, bra straps, silk blouses already sweaty, sat a saturnine similarly aged observer: one Henry Schlesinger, 22. Where the lights were low and there were constant spasmodic flashes of color: red, blue, green, violet, yellow—a strobe cycling quickly through a series of colors and flash-illuminating somehow to unsettling effect twisting thinly-robed bodies and thick-browed, arch-browed, amped-up Western young men in predictable clothes wanting to get behind any of a number of nubile, contorting women and thrust, feeling a sense of yearning and urgency, intoxicated; perspiring primates sharply watched by he who in a full room was at his most alone, who was in a state of deep sullen inebriation. Who seemed to feel night seeping inexorably, lazily into dawn, who was thinking the dumbfucks he'd seen too much of in America were here with him too, dirty dancing and mistreating the locals, and being "normal" and getting into it (losing themselves, living in the moment, unhindered by contemplation or self-awareness), something Henry could not as easily do (which was why he was always having to drink more to compensate, until inevitably he'd overdone it—and then he drank more maybe; despondent, envious, introspective, quietly watching, judging, sipping whatever it might be, a biya Chang, at the bar confident and paid no attention to (when not himself drunkenly dance-floor-mock-fucking)).

———— ⁙ ————

In childhood a simply structured area he called "the fort" had been constructed for him by his father, utilizing a number of wooden pallets, on the side of the carport of the last of the three houses he'd grown up in. The entrance was in the backyard; at the other end, facing the street, was one upright pallet for a half-wall; the floor was one layer of pallets; the thin wood of the carport constituted one wall while pallets lined up against the massive trunks of a row of aspens that towered and often shed over the space constituted the other. It was tucked narrow between the knotty wall of the vehicle-shelter and the old, scratched lower girth of numerous always-swaying gargantuan trees, a row of kin near which was a row of eight-foot or so scratchy bushes favored by bees and wasps and on warm days buzzing with them that, behind low chicken-wire, were rooted at the forward boundary of the auto shelter. He recalled observing clandestinely from there, many a morning, afternoon and early evening over years, the public that came into his limited view; reading, while he paced, *The Master of Ballantrae*. He remembered enjoying that secret, nearly claustrophobic spot, which eventually— though its upkeep would have been easy for someone suited to the task—fell into disrepair.

———◦((◦))◦———

When he was a child unwanted visitors who seemed to exist only in his psyche would appear sometimes late at night: Jim the male, who was completely green, and companion Marsha, who was solely red, whose names he knew telepathically. They were featureless, merely contoured blobs, an eerie surreal pair most likely hallucinated that would not dematerialize, it was communicated wordlessly, until he had made his bed, topped by a thick red and green tasseled blanket, in a to them (or him) basically perfect manner—a task he attempted and reattempted at length and frustratingly but never seemed to achieve, not to their satisfaction; though despite this they, and he with them, would at length disappear, would dissipate imperceptibly into oblivion, an oblivion that in his case was no doubt unconsciousness. And in the morning he remembered only a slow, horrifying cycle of assiduously making and remaking his bed, concerned with symmetry and smoothing every ripple in his bedding, a series of memories of flattening the blanket and arranging its tassels so they were all identically oriented. He remembered it, with an internal shudder, as an eternity, an inescapable, inexplicable permanent reality, though at least drew some comfort from the knowledge that they—the visage- and voiceless intruders who had the power to impose their will by thought, by just their presence—were temporarily gone, while he remained on the earthly plane.

They could have been a dream, but he didn't remember the experiences as dreams, literal nightmares. Also as a child he had, over the years, reoccurring flying dreams, and they were pleasant—the one he experienced most often actually being one in which he floated. In these the setting, spectators, varied but the method and manner of flying—levitating—did not. Usually or always being the only one who could he was able to float/fly (a wonderful sensation) with a limited ability to maneuver that he was able to improve upon through trial and error. He could begin to levitate whether lying down, sitting, or standing and it seemed to be a mostly mentally controlled capability, physically to a lesser degree and more vaguely. The main dangers (very real when he was situated out of doors)—other than landing incorrectly (e.g. with too much force)—were power lines and sudden losses of altitude for which he was to blame (typically floating involved ascending or descending but rarely coasting), both potentially big problems for an inexperienced flier, more so the higher they'd intentionally or unintentionally risen.

———⋙«❶»⋘———

Sometimes he used to involuntarily imagine he saw Pa, Pap, his near-forgotten father, imagine random people were him—a passerby, a man he passed and barely glimpsed, a stranger, a vagabond of similar age and facial features—disconcertingly, and for a brief time be utterly convinced; and an ineffable feeling would go through him then as if spinally.

He used to think Henry was partially deaf; so as a little

boy he was subjected to an aural test in a mobile audiologic clinic in a mall parking lot, a test that found him to have perfect hearing (maybe though he'd developed into a selective hearer). He was a man who used to threaten to kill himself or his wife fairly frequently, often due to not having marijuana or anyone who would or could give him money for some. Childhood was when, due to his father, he first met drug people, the real fucked up kind with crack-/meth-created stubs of teeth and worse-for-wear druggie girlfriends—many folks of that ilk being friends, acquaintances, associates of his (or associates of associates).

He, Pap of prior days, was likely alive; Henry had it on good evidence he'd completed recently an intensive drug rehabilitation program, and there were indications he was perhaps in Northern Florida someplace, holding a steady job. Prior to that there was something about a stay in a mental hospital. Before that Henry'd learned he'd had facial reconstructive surgery in Orange County. FL. Henry's mother discovered this from a medical bill he forwarded to her house in lieu of paying.

In his final memory of him he was screaming from his second-story bedroom window waving a Beretta; meanwhile Henry, his mother and brother left the house and the maniac—then, as typical, childlike, pathetic—in the dusty brown AMC Concord parked in the driveway, none of them ever to see him again. It was some years before they lived there; then, his mentally ill male progenitor's whereabouts long unknown, they moved back in.

In those days the black mustache he never shaved though trimmed was skirted always by a five o'clock shadow. His thin, angular face was weathered and scarred. His nose had been broken several times and a smashed cheekbone had never properly been fixed, leaving the visage a bit lopsided. Kids called him Dumbo all through grade school because his ears were comically too large for his head. Of those teeth that hadn't been knocked out they were black with decay many of them and at varying stages of slow destruction. Some were rotted to the nub. This is the reason he never opened his mouth when he smiled. (Nor, to memory, did he ever truly smile; but, mostly for family pictures posed for in small portrait studios at the backs of department stores, he on occasion forced onto his face a near facsimile of a smile.) And it could be deduced his hating to eat in public was not unrelated. Maybe too he hated to see a bunch of stupid cows do the same.

A man who seemed little concerned with personal hygiene, there was really nothing left that could be called teeth, just charcoal-hued ruins, or rotting outgrowths that were color combinations otherworldly or in context repellent, and his wavy jet-black hair, kept on the longer side, was always greasy in a way that could be discerned from a distance. On church mornings he halfheartedly disguised the aroma of a week's sweat with cheap Avon musk.

His father, while in his life, had been the only parent he spent much time with, early childhood excluded. At the general hospital where he was a pill-thieving CNA he came in only sporadically, whenever a need/desire to work and a certain level of sobriety corresponded. He was overqualified for the job and kept it for years, until a superior discovered he was forging his own prescriptions for Vicodin, Valium et al.

From then on he was rarely employed and, Henry being home-schooled, the twain of them (three once Henry's brother was born) spent most of their time at home while Henry's mother worked, Henry accompanying him as he ran errands, generally procuring pot or pills, or watching TV downstairs while he got stoned throughout the day. At some point, in part to fund her husband's psychological addiction to marijuana, the matriarch of the family got a second job. Her two incomes were enough to pay the rent and support the family, but even working all the time Henry's parents found she couldn't manage to fully subsidize his voracious habit, and Pap always needed his ganja and his prescription drugs, and even to always have Coca-Cola, or he would throw a sort of tantrum. For the pills he drove to hospitals and health clinics in a hundred-mile radius, conning doctors (a fake oral click was his only con in such endeavors Henry was aware of, and most of the time it strangely worked). But when there was nothing left in the house to pawn, he turned to his beleaguered wife for money to buy pot; for a few bucks for Coke too, which he drank only from a glass with ice, if the two-liter bottle in the fridge had run dry.

Whenever he was mellow though (and he had to have his herb and soda in order to be) he was fun, often hanging out with his elder son. After a half-hour upstairs with his bong he might come downstairs coughing deeply and ask Henry if he wanted to play "war." The funnest and most involving of the three versions of this was played with newspaper cutouts of soldiers about two inches wide and four inches long. Henry'd have one army and he'd have the other, the armies having some obvious physical disparity (like one having pointy heads as if World War I Germans). Ammo was newspaper rolled up into big balls for bombs or tiny pellets for grenades, plus individual soldiers could resort to hand-to-hand combat if proximity allowed, resulting in random minor amputations (as opposed to more serious ones or casualties caused by explosives). They'd also play using plastic soldiers, and, in the backyard, using the large leaves of weeds. This was something he had done as a boy with his brothers and sisters. An oil painting hanging in the living room he was fond of depicted Henry's father and aunt and uncle playing "leaf war" in a windy field in Somewhereberg, Bumfuck, in the deep South, his hometown. Who'd painted it Henry didn't recall or he never said. Had he even said it was of his siblings and him, or was it simply a piece of art he'd found of children engaged in seemingly the same pastime—or had he lied?

Games of war and eating the peanut butter, marshmallow and banana sandwiches he often made that were much liked by both of them, and which he had been eating since childhood, accounted for many of the happy memories Henry had of him. Being driven around in the front seat of the shiny, fire-engine red Toyota Tercel he had bought used—and that he not infrequently lost because he had no memory of parking it due to how fucked up he was—when he ran "errands" made up many of the recollections of which Henry was not so fond. These errands were primarily pawning things at shops along a drag dense with such establishments, hitting up hospitals/clinics, and going with him to buy weed; or to hang out with Henry's uncle, his brother, at an apartment near the aforementioned boulevard, in a slummy neighborhood.

Henry remembered too his stories of an ignominious military career, of ten years of recklessness; imagining blows that caused injuries followed by scars, marks of adventurous and haphazard living. Resentment for spending what felt like half his preadolescence reading in or staring at characterless waiting rooms or sitting on a couch somewhere watching him make sly transactions with his "friends," or just waiting in the car, then coming home and quietly cursing into the walls of his room because the TV and the Nintendo were gone; resentment for many reasons. And that his father kept pets and abused his reptile, a monitor, and his two dogs. The pet of the former species died after a particularly cruel round of torture, torture in the tub, water punishment and pinches met with further-infuriating snaps. (He hurt the lizard because it would bite him when he moved it to and from its glass cell to be cleaned, and while it was being washed.) Also he maltreated Henry's beloved cat, black with white paws, which without cause he permanently chased away with rocks—it hadn't even been on the property—with equal disregard for feline and firstborn (an event that must have made a lasting impression on both).

And he remembered after spankings and belt whippings, always over some trivial infraction, saying "I hate him" over and over in his room, chanting it, rage building with the repetition, a rage for which the reiteration of the phrase was conversely his only conscious release—a release that might not have augmented the anger if he'd been able to raise his voice.

Henry had had, before he was a grown man, two near-drowning experiences—one in childhood, one in early adulthood. The first, at Christian family camp, occurred when he was around ten years old: he was internally again in the reservoir not far from shore when he recollected yelling for help (his voice coming out weak), his panic having been suppressed as best as possible as long as possible, to longtime childhood crush Jodi (who would turn out to be the first girl he ever fingered, and the two fingers that smelled like her he didn't wash awhile but occasionally smelled throughout the night; who earlier (when they were children) he had long silly phone conversations and exchanged notes with; who in high school (they went to the same one) became known for her excessive application of glitter and being promiscuous; who had a kid in her early twenties, the product of a year-long marriage, and became a stripper, as she was when Henry hung out with her shortly after getting back from Thailand, when they went to a diner and then her house and she was sitting on her bed about to let him fuck her but he said "I thought we could make out first," and she responded "How sweet," which kind of bothered him for some reason, and then it came up that in Thailand he had had sex with a lot of hookers and that he hadn't always worn a condom. "That's good to know" she said sarcastically. And then they didn't fuck), who waved and splashed near the strand with her friend, oblivious or not taking him seriously.

He had gone out far (for him) with a boogie-boarding

adult and near-adult who were, unlike him, competent swimmers (he'd had swimming lessons that didn't take) and, uncomfortable because of the distance and his known poor aquatic ability, he began to swim back alone; halfway to shore both legs cramped up, one after the other, so he was immobilized and started to panic. Subconsciously he found himself imagining a quite early death in a lake at family camp close to touching depth for his five-foot frame, with someone known to him most of his blink-duration life (like land) very near, Jodi, who along with her counterpart (both merry, one-piece-garbed) and the two recreating behind him—one of whom saved him as the animal started to think it was about to go under, then end (experiencing as its brain died a bliss state otherworldly)—were the only people in sight.

The other event, when he was twenty-one, occurred just two weeks before he was to leave Thailand. He was in a small boat in the river Kwai at night, a river the bottom of which was covered with old bones he imagined his own joining. He'd capsized the rowboat he was in along with a friend by, because of his inebriation, standing up in it. "I can't swim. I can't swim," he had said to his companion across from him, Jasmine, a skilled swimmer who was dog-paddling, as he struggled to keep his head above the undulating water. Having maneuvered to where he was underneath a house-boat he saved himself by jumping and after several failed attempts clinging with his fingernails to the rivets on one of the wide plastic sections of pipe beneath the floating cabin roped to shore and then managing to pull himself up onto its deck of adjoined planks. It required thereafter the totality of his strength to pull the rowboat in against the brisk current, and one of the oars (for which he was charged 3000 baht) was lost to the fast-moving water. Plastic sandals for the walk back to his own floating cabin, a ways downriver, were graciously given to him, unasked, by the married French man and Thai woman whose dwelling he and his friend passed as they walked the road back to their weekend abode. Solomon, drunk, commented on Jasmine's massive tits that evening, later. Colleague Solomon was a former Daytona Beach detective; he always carried a switchblade and often flashed it at Henry (and there was also always a threat in his eyes when theirs briefly made contact). He had a jovial side but his face often betrayed a certain subsurface meanness; had a shaved head and a white and gray goatee, never not neatly trimmed. Within a bar a short while after meeting Jasmine Henry'd expressed his desire to kiss her, and though she had a boyfriend she responded to his advances, and they winded up making out at a famous Bangkok monument in the middle of a roundabout, he groping her huge tits as they frenched at length, his body pressing hers against the tall bronze sculpture, teenage Thais screaming from the windows of passing vehicles.

⸺•«(●)»•⸺

Hailstorms in July and five or ten minutes later clear skies and seventy-five, fifteen minutes later ninety. One seventh month that was the weather...

One February nineteenth he was kind of hungover, kind of weak-feeling; lethargic, supremely lethargic. Another night spent at the bar the previous night, a Thursday, and too much money spent, despite his intention to never do this again (get too drunk/spend a lot of money at a bar or bars), despite having done so just two and a half weeks earlier, not even having stuck to his resolution a month. He was eating orange Tic-Tacs and drinking tap water. Everything seemed dull, duller than it usually did, his mind was dull. He felt he might, without being able to catch, to stop himself, begin to cry or laugh, in a sick way, about nothing—as he had on returning home that morning at a little past three a.m. In addition to all this he was sleep-deprived, for the second day in a row; he hadn't managed regardless of being drunk and tired (but feeling neither) to fall asleep until about five, and had had to be up for work before noon.

***

Henry—though he'd once come to believe he would likely never, told himself could never, unite, be in an extended intimate relationship, with a woman who was both sufficiently physically attractive to and was sufficiently compatible with him—had always been doing a lot better than a lot of people, in a survival sense if none other, yet he not often enough thought of and all too rarely properly, fully, appreciated this. People (in general/his neck of the woods—a colloquialism he disliked) were always thinking about themselves first and too frequently wanting—wanting what weren't needs; wanting more, more, no matter what they had. And didn't experience enough removal from ant-level and mind-centered goings-on, enough appreciation of the good (at least in a sense of the word having to do with necessities, or better yet a spiritual sense—which objectivity might develop, as well as perchance the notion, a truth, that all were one; the requisite being a occurrence that led to insight).

<hr />

He and a Nigerian guy he'd been hanging out with in Hangzhou, whom he met at the restaurant Henry ate at almost every night, went downtown for a Christmas night lay and away from main avenues they discovered a hair salon (which many of the brothels in China doubled as) occupied by two women who were willing to fuck for money before the boss came back, one about forty and the other sexy and twenty, with shortish spiky hair and a slim body.

Henry said he was only interested in fucking the latter. His acquaintance agreed and each couple went to one of the areas in back demarcated by curtains and thin dividers. The Nigerian finished in five minutes or so but Henry wasn't able to with a condom on despite how hot she was, fantasy stuff. Below and facing him, her bra removed and shirt pulled up to her armpits to expose two wonderful breasts, she finally told him he could take the rubber off, but he still didn't come anytime soon and didn't want to. He stood fucking her hard then with subsiding vigor, hard then force subsiding, sometimes shivering involuntarily because of how good it was all-around, looking at her hard-nippled little tits and pussy with a little triangle of pubes above it as his latex-wrapped hard-on went in and out and his testicles slapped audibly against her, admiring her perfect figure and face and occasionally grabbing one or both firm b-cups, taking in her body while he enjoyed it, while subconsciously marveling at suddenly having a super-sexy whore whose tight trimmed ideal pussy was between legs spread wide his to pound until he came (by which time both of them were thoroughly tuckered), who easily and superbly received his thoroughgoing fuck. But after finishing, when they were out on the street, Henry experienced the known fear of having contracted HIV (he had not intended to not use protection, but at the point she suggested he remove the raincoat his will not to was already gone). "You don't have AIDS" his comrade consoled him as they walked away down an alley, to a main road to find a cab. There were still light bruises on his upper thighs, from her thighs, four days later.

<hr />

In Thailand once, in a still-busy Western restaurant on Khao Sarn, he had at the last minute—after trying to find a regular girl or a working one he liked more till something like four a.m.—settled for a whore in her mid or late thirties with a very sweet disposition who had, he was pleased to discover (after, the moment the door to his apartment was shut, she quickly removed her clothes), despite a slight amount of cellulite, a very nice, petite body. He fucked her with the lights on that early morning wearing a condom but couldn't come and she said he could take it off, and some time later he did come except before he could pull out and she jumped up practically while he was still coming yelling "Are you crazy?" "You don't have AIDS. You don't have AIDS" she said as she went to the wetroom to rinse the semen out of her. And he thought *I am crazy*, that was a further demonstration, and thought *I don't have AIDS, I don't have AIDS*, trying to assure himself as she been trying to assure herself, though he realized that she didn't have AIDS to her knowledge based on her having done so, just as he didn't as far as he knew. And together they walked down the gray dirty street a short ways to a drugstore where he purchased a day-after pill he gave her along with taxi fare.

Once—in the city that was home to West Lake and to him for roughly six months—he was kicked out of a sleazy club at around four a.m., having tried to pick up a girl or find a whore for some time (pathetically), despite the fact he'd earlier that day patronized a prostitute. Going through the lobby on his way out, drunk and with a full bladder, as a way of expressing his feelings toward the establishment—frustrated, only minimally present—he spontaneously decided to take a leak on a couch against a wall in the peopleless foyer. His dick out, about finished (having made a point to distribute the piss across all the cushions), out of the club walked an unimposing fellow, an employee, his eyes (which locked a half-moment with Henry's) wide with shock. Member put back in his pants, left unzipped, Henry walked briskly out, away; but about a block distant his arm was grasped by the same employee, wild-eyed, who was trying to pull Henry back toward the club for punishment sure to be quite negative. Upon being given a fully desperate, half feral look that said he would assault the man to escape, the latter let go and Henry, shaken, relieved, continued quickly toward home, his head full of gratitude for his freedom and ideas of what might have been in store for him had he been seized.

...Remembering a story he'd been told once in the former Siam he saw with his mind's eye an American soldier in Pattaya— drunk, woozy—stumble out of a bedbug-ridden brothel and then pass out, his penis already imperceptibly rotting and soon to be gangrened-looking from an STD acquired in the past few hours. Saw himself without looking throwing a beer mug in a dark bar. The middleaged Chinese man sitting across from him, with whom he'd been communicating with difficulty, just stared, his face reading complete contempt, lack of intimidation. (Henry left soon thereafter, drunk and seen to be sociopathic.) Saw the driver of a tuk-tuk speeding along a Krung Thep thoroughfare glancing back at him with an expression that said he was both ill at ease and found his passenger reprehensible.

———◉———

He sat in a big-chain diner, his purple cotton sleeves rolled up, on a Wednesday dull-skied afternoon. He drank coffee, bottles of Budweiser, smoked Camels in the hazy back smoking area, smelling of it all probably, simultaneously tasting the three on his tongue; was drawn into conversation with old men alcoholics, one missing teeth and weary, the other in black sunglasses and a Quicksilver cap, both frequently grabbing smokes from where their packs lay on their respective tables and first talking about trouble (in general)

then the World Series (Red Sox versus Cardinals, Sox un-
defeated; Henry didn't give a fuck) then liquor and sickness
and then the quick consumption of two cups of java and a
beer had him starting to sweat (partly because his body tem-
perature had risen and the room-temperature restaurant was
so much warmer than the end-of-October outside). Their
waitress had child-bearing hips (as one of them had commented), a bounty of breasts, a lovely face, pulled-tightly-
back brunette hair, was watched walking back and forth
attending the small smoking section. "Do you know her?"
asked the more garrulous of the twain, the man in sunglasses,
a lot of him obscured, once blond beard almost wholly white.

"No, I don't know anyone..."

"Well she's sure looking at *you*." His eyebrows went high.
"Nothing wrong with that. She's got a nice body." The man
put his hand to his mouth in the way people did when im-
parting secrets. "The old man's a cop," he whispered.

What was he talking about? Henry chose not to respond.
The other old man (not that it mattered) was not a cop,
was far from looking it. Henry was mildly perplexed, and
remained that way, and soon needed to depart. "Goodbye
gentlemen," he said in a way that was too good-natured or
formal. He had to get on the coming bus. Aboard, he was
as observant as usual, but engaged himself in nothing other
than observation, and only paid attention to the occupants
of the bus, the awkward transportation machine, and its mo-
tions, and not vehicles and people and structures, scenery
outside the big bus windows as he might've if he were not
feeling ill, stomach sick, body wishing it weren't being jerked
around; then, briskly tackling the sidewalks, navigating the

mid-afternoon people downtown, he got to work on time but very hot, wishing he didn't have to work, didn't have to sit in a gray-walled cubicle conducting phone surveys that day; feeling small sticking beads of sweat forming on his forehead, emerging from pores in and between beginnings of wrinkles; during the shift becoming aware of a disagreeable smell of perfume and cigarettes like from a middleaged woman who didn't much shower.

⸻ ◈ ⸻

On the bus south...he was tired; *I feel like shit* he'd more than once said to himself. The bus was at full capacity. At the first stop there were cows on knolls of dead grass. Then they were winding through tall forest; then, again, there were bare mountains to each side; then hillocks spotted with wisps of weeds; then he got his second wind. He appeared, plausibly, intelligent and alert, but pale, eyes darkly encircled, perhaps sickly. A child, male, kicked the back of his seat. The kicks were sometimes violent surprises that jolted him from pseudo-sleep, but eventually they ceased. He knew though that the boy was perhaps asleep and that the nuisance might resume. *How much of the trip to Modesto will he be joining me for?* wondered Henry. *Will he be replaced by another alike?* Beside him was a big older woman whose body was continually threatening to overflow her seat until she adjusted herself (so far without fail), who twitched with a spasm of the shoulder every so often—perhaps not a natural quirk but a consequence of discomfort, of Greyhound special misery.

186

Modesto they were scheduled to arrive in at 5:25; they'd reached Roseburg some three hours prior; Medford was next, at 6:40. So started a long journey, one in a series which, as life, went on and on. Adventure called the bold, and shifts in personality—like those of the tectonic plates, frequent but not accurately able to be forecast—would doubtless follow; for life was also a series of modifications, both intentional and otherwise, in reaction to past experiences.

He hated people he was thinking, sometimes (sometimes superficially). Including and at the moment especially the amazing-looking girl (sexually speaking) two rows behind him and a seat to the right who he presently heard talking—some of her words but none of her sentences discernible. Who through two looks (only one was necessary) and her briefly observed demeanor told him she knew how sexy she was, how attention-drawing (many as beautiful did, not as many let on). And he hated her not for this unremarkable awareness, less so because of her looks or easy readability, but due to the fact that he knew, knew quite certainly, that no matter what surfeit of dislike he would likely have for her if he got to know her he would nonetheless be unable to turn off an attraction to the feminine cloak she operated in; to her prominent hipbones; shown sunned soft stomach; small breasts; probably exquisite vagina. He would nonetheless want to do things to her, and derive a great deal of pleasure, satisfaction, from doing so were he able. He would be powerless.

(And was powerless. And of this he was aware. And hated people for it. And to a lesser degree, less perceivably, hated himself.)

187

And, it really could go unsaid, he disliked most personalities he encountered too. And drama, making unnecessary waves. (He appeared the restrained young gentleman.)

Decorated crosses appeared beside freeways, just on the edge of forest, where little boys or girls—or grownups, some perhaps in their prime—were killed by vehicles big, small or in between, being driven by people careful or inattentive, old or young. And though Henry had just been thinking *I wish he wasn't alive* and wishing the legs were cut off of the presently unoffending child seated directly behind him, he didn't really want that to happen, and would not harm a child in most realistic scenarios, not intentionally, nor for that matter wish one any true harm. *I am a thinking man* he thought, and almost below consciousness could imagine himself a functionally dressed urbane older man (because he was vain. And there was nothing of substance in vanity. Vanity was a deathly quality). Though dying a little every moment he felt he remained a decent human specimen (albeit nuanced, troubled)...and hoped to remain such as long as he possessed a modicum of mental health.

<hr />

He was thinking about the sort of makeup young girls often wore and the way they frequently wore it, lipstick very red or brightly colored that was typically thickly applied, resulting in an appearance clownish or tawdry...At the moment his sleep deprivation was severe; his mind kept wandering down seemingly uncorrelated alleys... In the airport he met

"Kevin," a Shanghainese—needed advice was provided by him, (more) fear instilled. (He was in Portland about to fly to China, to the city Kevin was from.)

Henry's lids were like pulp, or steel, impossible to keep open long enough to read a page... He was hungry, he... planned to eat another pudding cup...planned to eat every meal on the plane and to drink as many free beers as he could; planned to quit smoking on the plane; planned to sleep on the plane (would have regardless of his plans), aboard which he went (abroad) to die again (to his life in America).

———◉———

A Chinese boy brandished paper claws on one hand at a counterpart who occupied a posterior seat. With a familiar ding on went the LAVATORY AFT sign—or it was turbulence, the seatbelt light. The aircraft was about at the Sea of Okhotsk, meaning he was approximately twenty-four hundred miles and less than eight hours away from Shanghai— where he hoped his bag and ride were waiting.

III

THIS EXPERIENCE OF the interior of this fortress, this Oxon, as it performed what according to Keen was one of its functions, contrary to what he'd had in the way of expectation, was not exclusively visual, interactive, a succession of scenes ostensibly physical that formed around or before him that he could step into, the known origin of which was his mind, and neither was it a series of palpable pictures. No, instead it was predominantly stimuli foreign in source and content—scenes and images seemingly telepathically transmitted, outside of the spatial—and not generally pleasant as it streamed through his consciousness in the void, seeming to replace his with that of some other (if, corporeally, "he" (meaning he knew no longer what) currently existed anywhere anymore; perhaps the vacuum he was in was beyond the mortal realm), as if he was tapped into someone else's mind, someone fairly similar but of a different time, who had had a different life, whose thoughts were despairing, not sane; and it was mostly thoughts, brief tales, glimpses, that since the onset he'd been receiving, thoughts made manifest, thoughts like those of a sentient computer overloaded, not optimally operating, infected; indeed perhaps it was not the consciousness of another human being but of some sort of machine. A sensory stream the aggregate sensation of which was that of a nightmare, in this case a nightmare he couldn't wake from (if he were asleep, which he felt certain he wasn't) or make stop. It was like his entry into Oxon or his journey up the silver staircase that from his mind it'd manifested had killed him and he inhabited now a Hell worse than that he'd left, been born into; or perhaps he'd been trapped in some manner of living chamber that'd decided or was designed to drive its captive crazy. But these cerebrations of his did not stop the flow of the alien ones or elucidate the situation...

Some of the stimuli, some of it having seemingly been downloaded into his brain, may have been coming from this Henry, figure fictitious or once real. Stimuli like seeing and hearing manifestations of other people's unpleasant thoughts, like he had been given windows to their unhealthy minds (made crazed by the minds themselves), sad, mad psyches set to unhappiness.

The ongoing ordeal had, he realized, made the reasons for the hypothetical humans' mental illness seem all the more understandable; his having been force-fed an enormous serving of it had rendered, for Orlan the entity in eternity, a sort of common Earth-situated horror more tangible than ever.

It occurred to Orlan, now, that he was maybe a reincarnation of Henry. (Immediately he disliked the notion and felt if so he'd little if at all improved.)

———⊙———

Nothing mattered, and everything. Forms were born and died but these were vessels of the physical befuddling world, beneath which was immortality. Everything was fine and always had been. The only thing that was ever temporarily not fine was anything anyone ever did out of malice (especially if the malice was undeserved) to one's fellow organisms. The dreamlike (or was it a dream? or was his whole life essentially?) kaleidoscope ever before his open eyes—physical eyes that seemed more than that—perpetually altering, was fine, okay, alright, and in fact better than that: a great gift to be thankful for. All life almost seemed beautiful, glorious (a word he seldom used)—sometimes, in moments of elucidation, seemed wonderful—because it was life; though heinous acts were perpetrated in this life, by some of those living more blindly, apathetically, acts that seemed symptomatic of (certain states of) life, even if they were the price to pay it did not negate the worthwhileness of life, of the life of a puny drop-in-the-ocean specimen of the species H. sapiens; and one ought to empathize with the human sufferers of human-induced plights over the ages, to imagine, to try to feel to the degree possible the horrors of the Inquisition, the Holocaust, of various genocides and wars and experience substantial deep sorrow, through which compassion, understanding, would be increased (for the purpose of the brief existence given to individuals was to learn and love, to learn to love (fellow people, creatures)). And as knowledge was multiplied members of the genus could attain the feeling he seemed to be feeling presently, of peace, acceptance, gratitude, captivation, aesthetic appreciation, even a sort of underlying love, especially toward those he respected and admired, some of whom seemed to be imperfect humanity in a kind of perfection. So many unfortunately yet lived in emptiness, in false escapes of emptiness (like viewcube, foundationally instable romantic relationships, drugs, food, pets, sports, memorizing and regurgitating trivialities, shopping, partying, holidays, events, anniversaries), ways of hiding it from oneself, temporarily leaving, attention turned/tuned to somewhere other than one's perceived and ultimately self-created hell of mind, life. So many people wanted, needed, inner tranquility; a multitude didn't even know it to try to seek it out. However the bliss was there always before them, the sad scurrying creatures of small, suffocating Earth (no, not so small—populated unsustainably). But they could, if they saw this, grasped it, know happiness in soaping and scrubbing a pot or journeying in their imaginations into a space between fence posts or the glare on the viewcube (rather than as usual being hypnotized by the (social) pro-gramming ad-punctuated that emanated from the ubiqui-tous appliance a great number of men and women devoted, often unconsciously, the lion's share of their free time to, the electric box that was the focal point of most living rooms and supplied a constant buzz of typically thought-suppressing inanity (not that thought was good or bad in and of itself, thought though commonly being the mind's own stream of gabble)). A large part of the human race was either be-ing deprived by forces inhuman of what no human ought to be or else enduring a futile unhappiness characterized by cancers, the worst of which did not attack the body but the soul—entering in through apparatuses of the physical shell and being churned into disease through the mind, everyone's inner saboteur in a world of external ones, individual and conglomerative. Many regarded their lives as mostly misery, discontentment, or as a sort of long static melancholy; spent them like children in pursuit of fleeting fleshly/creature pleasures, of validation, trying to find felicity where it never was (not really or not for long), trying to get their way. But they had always been beings made of light, visible through light, incomprehensibly complex entities of infinite potential comprised of differently combined particles, stardust, meant for the light, meant to know, and accordingly (contrary to the saying "ignorance is bliss") enjoy—never, certainly not to be healthy, detest—the lightness of existences of brevity among the myriad compositions of their kind and kinds other that radiated in common with consciousness; to (try to) not hurt and to appreciate (the symphony, not evil architects), to realize the commonality of life and the wonder of existence on a spinning ball in a great vastness on which were conditions right for the thriving of the species; to learn and experience and know the beyond awaited and it was not a bad but good thing (if one was not at heart, speaking of their soul, so much *bad* as *good*, to use subjective, problematic words justified by the simplistic ideas they represented) and to look into the beyond of space (where there were certainly other organisms, abundant, at great distances) and at their own planet and know there were innumerable marvels and questions and likely, eventually, answers. Orlan, a living thing with a name and with a body in ongoing, subtly progressing decay—tangible shelter of an essence intangible, making him plausible, palpable, functional on the plane he occupied with the rest of the Earth humans with elemental bodies—had looked into the darkness deeply and was therefore all the more comprehending of the light that he was fortunate to see before the end of/for the last light seen in natural life, actually just after, between existence in the setting familiar and somewhere that is not a place, not physically, life less describable lived timelessly not so much anywhere as everywhere; he was also more comprehending of the dark, of the falseness within and without, more recognizing of the symptoms of an illness that could make life seem an evil.

⸺◉⸺

But in the end, sadly, despite all, any enlightenment and despite and because of experience, Henry did not like it on Earth, could not bring himself with finality to hope for the best, and looked forward to death; dreaded waking, the day ahead (just as Orlan longed to depart Oxon, Earth (which was perhaps not Oxon's location, if it had one), longed for death—if he wasn't already dead). So he felt due to the person he'd become, because of the way the world had become, because of the injustice, the lunacy of the way things were, how he was treated in the nation of his birth. His prognosis for and view of the people—the masses (at least in his neck of the woods) he had a general resentment for undying—was a negative one. He'd been permanently poisoned, whether he wished or even felt temporarily otherwise or not. The destruction of all, those of his fatherland first, first himself, he knew was ultimately his desire. (And he had sometimes fantasized about a continent-sized blender, reaching into space, in which the entire population of the planet had been trapped, the uppermost of them pressed against its lid. And then the massive 'puree' button was pressed and the rotors of the device whirred rapidly. And after a few moments all that remained of the species was a substance that bore a resemblance to strawberry jam filling an absurd, gargantuan appliance.) Oh well and so it goes he wanted to see burn all that industrial society had polluted the world and made it ugly with, prior to the eradication of the people (though it was especially those of his own country—and its treasonous government, the well-being of whose subjects was not a priority—he wanted to go; the populace and system he had to live with, day in, day out): vehicles and skyscrapers and unsightly gray-exhaling factories first (and shopping centers, streetlights, telephone poles/lines and parking garages; rectangle after rectangle of commercial property), the mean, the stupid, the insulated, those who cared ultimately only about themselves running screaming ablaze through the streets of some variety of charred postindustrial hell; he was done with it, them, the dream of horror. And even if the nightmare became a different sort of dream other than a worse one it would nonetheless be a nightmare of a kind, his anyway, so it was only natural he should wish to wake from and forget it. He might want one moment to make the zoo more pleasant, one moment to wreak havoc in it, but to hear the deathly wails of the hominids and see the crumbling of their structures all around them, the wiping clean of any sign of their pitiful poisonous civilization from the globe, what was commonly called progress, was his ultimate desire. No more ugly people, ugly places—everything consumed in a conflagration.

He was after all a prisoner, slave, rat in a trap—and being a captive of the pen potentially wonderful but instead a loathed dystopia was enough for him to not want to remain inside it. Instead he would likely paint a few beautiful and horrifying pictures of the trap (that a very few people would see prior to the paintings' destruction and that it will have been almost pointless to have created), hang them in it, and then hang himself (or otherwise shove off, the evil farce over).

———— ((◦)) ————

Orlan realized his power probably was and all along had been, in Oxon, godlike (but was he his waking self or dream self (both of which were in a manner of speaking real, different sides of him, like his drunk self)?—he felt the latter); and he worried about not being able to control himself, as god, dream self, omnipotent creator (of an illusion). Why could he not escape Oxon? Was he disallowing himself? Was it because he was asleep and, as was often the case, could not wake of his own volition? He would much rather, than endlessly teleporting through his subconscious (he supposed that was what was happening, the explanation for the succession of dreams experienced with reality's vividness), be free from the vagaries of the better-left-cobwebbed corners of his mind, his boundaryless wandering imagination—ideally permanently. He would rather not be a prisoner of a structure—unless it was a construct?—that defied everything he knew by being what he'd deemed impossible, that left it exclusively up to him to haunt himself. If in fact he was, as he speculated, most likely dreaming Oxon, its strange simply dressed female occupants (that seemed typical of him), then it was also likely a dream from which he did not wish himself to (easily) escape. Yes—yes it was, had to've been, all a dream. For how had he come to be at the place where the wind shook the many green shrubs on the wide plain, where nothing was visible in any direction at any distance but more bushes, an endless field of leafy knobs rustled by whistling gusts, and more plain—where he walked into what at first was the invisible metallic exterior of the otherworldly void that allowed him entry and then, with the aid of an unknown woman, attractive, oddly clothed, ensnared him (but only till his own mind opted to release him? would then the foreign fortress disappear? would he find himself in bed?)?